LANDOVER
A TIME FOR CHANGE

I0623298

R.K. BRUMBALOW

Landover: A Time for Change
Copyright © 2024 R. K. Brumbalow

Paperback Book ISBN-13: 979-8-9896506-2-0
EBook ISBN-13: 979-8-9896506-3-7

This is a work of fiction. Names, characters, places, and incidents are a product of the author's imagination or are used fictitiously. Any resemblance to actual people, living or dead, or to businesses, companies, events, institutions, or locales is completely coincidental.

Cover design by Keith Brumbalow

Visit us at Kbrumwrites.com.

Dedication

This book is dedicated to my family, especially my wife, Carol, who has been very patient while I worked on it. I trust it is one of more to come. I want to thank may Savior, Jesus Christ, for giving me the ability to complete this task.

ALSO BY

R. K. BRUMBALOW

NON-FICTION

<u>I JUST GOT SAVED: WHAT HAVE I DONE?</u>

Chapter 1

"Good morning! Thank you for calling Landover. How may I direct your call?" Cheryl asked.

"Good morning," the refined voice on the other end responded. "I would like to speak with someone in equipment sales. Not just anyone," the caller insisted, "but the best you have."

"I can put you through to Jack Fisher, as he seems to be the only salesman in at the moment."

"That would be splendid."

Quite a departure from his last sales job, Jack Fisher had found his niche selling construction equipment in the DFW area. As a bright, ambitious young man in his late twenties he knew what he wanted out of life and wouldn't change anything …yet.

Jack's phone rang as he was combing through his project folders in his lap, sorting them by dollar amount. He cleared his throat, picked up the receiver, and answered, "Sales, this is Jack. How can I help you?"

"Mr. Fisher, I understand you're the best," the caller greeted.

"Excuse me?" Jack responded, as he set the folders aside. He waited for the punch line, expecting this to be another adolescent prank from one of his buddies. He had not forgotten how, a few months back, his best friend Warren Phillips had called him and convinced Jack that Warren was an IRS agent. Before the call was over, Warren had Jack convinced he was going to jail and almost at the point of crying—something his coworkers still liked to kid him about.

"I told your receptionist I wanted to speak to the best equipment salesman there, and she recommended I speak with you. She was telling the truth, wasn't she?"

"I do okay," Jack answered, as he fell back into his chair and swiveled around to glance over at his first, recently acquired SOTY, or Salesman of the Year award. "How can I help you today, sir?"

"Mr. Fisher, I have an opportunity to grow my business and I'm looking for just the right equipment. I've been in this business a long time and have seen equipment come and go—most of it all the same—but your company offers some of the best."

"Yes, sir. We offer a wide range of options and capabilities to cover almost any need."

"Some of the equipment I have today is operating less than ideal, sub-par at best, and unlikely to ever achieve anything beyond mediocre performance. Therefore, my need is rather immediate and was hoping you would have some recommendations."

"Can I have your name, please?" Jack grabbed his pen and prepared to write.

"Oh, forgive me. My name is Edwards."

"I'll try to help you, Mr. Edwards, but you'll need to tell me a little about your business and your requirements."

"I'm really in a rush right now, Mr. Fisher, but I'll be in the area today and was hoping we could meet for lunch to discuss everything then. Would that be acceptable to you?"

Not exactly a sure thing, Jack thought, *but it would be nice to get out of here for a while. And, thanks to my company credit card, it'll be a free lunch.* "Sure, Mr. Edwards." Jack ran through a mental list of the local restaurants before settling on his favorite. "Are you familiar with McCardy's?"

"A great choice. It's one of my favorite places to dine."

"How about twelve-noon at McCardy's? I'll get there early and have a table waiting. Just ask for me at the hostess station."

"I'll see you then, and thank you, Mr. Fisher."

Jack hung up the phone and paused for a moment, with his hand still on the receiver. *Edwards. Where have I heard that name before? Radio? Television?*

Down the hall, Bill Redding, president of Landover, had gathered a few of his department managers in the boardroom for an impromptu meeting. Entering the boardroom last and closing the door behind him, Bill took his seat at the head of the table. At age 48, his stocky build exuded the youthful appearance of someone seven or eight years his junior. It helped that his hair showed no signs of turning gray or turning loose, and he showed no signs of slowing down.

Bill loved his job but was still getting used to the professional-management dress code; for, though it was still early in the morning, he already had his long sleeves rolled halfway up his forearms and his tie loosened. "Good morning, everyone," he began.

"Good morning," the group responded in a relaxed attitude.

"I know no one likes to have an unscheduled meeting first thing in the morning, but I wanted to get this done as soon as possible today. I'll try to be brief, so I don't hold you up any longer than necessary. First of all, I feel I should say, as I'm sure most of you are already aware, that business is good right now, and as a whole, our company is doing just fine. In fact, all the forecast numbers we've seen so far indicate the company is on its way to having its best year ever, particularly in equipment sales. Not bad for a company that has been well known for our outstanding service since day one, but not so much for equipment sales until now." The room was filled with subtle head nods and a few thumbs-up. "For the last several months, I have been working on a special project with our accountant, Walter Stevens, and we have found a few unsettling issues." The group stirred around a bit with a few whispered side blurbs. "Now don't read anything more into that than what I said, as it sounds worse than it really is. I'll repeat what I said before; the company is financially strong. We've just noticed some things going on that indicate change may be in order. I'm asking each of you to be on the lookout for any peculiar business dealings, whether internal or external, and should one of your staff bring you something out of the ordinary, don't draw any unnecessary attention to it. Keep the customer's best interest in mind, take care of the problem, and bring me the details."

"Is there anything in particular we should be looking for?" Glen asked.

"For you and your production department, probably not. Most of what we've seen surface so far has come through the service shop."

"What have you done now, Steven?" Glen joshed with the service manager.

"It was probably one of those inferior production pieces you put out that we had to go do some warranty work on," Steven bantered.

"Seriously, Bill," Glen added, "what kind of issues?"

"There have been a few irregular situations involving a handful of customers. Though Walter and I believe we've got our hands around it, there is still a little more investigating to be done. I know that's a very vague overview, and it sounds a little secretive, but I'm purposefully trying to minimize what information gets out. There is no need to speak of this to anyone outside this room. I'm sure this will be resolved within the next couple of weeks."

"Is there anything we can do to help?" Frank asked.

"Not at this time, Frank. I don't want to get any more people involved than I absolutely have to. Besides, I think we're about to get to the bottom of this. I've put together a tentative plan of action, which I'll implement once I'm satisfied the root cause has been identified. Does anyone else have a question?" The room was quiet. "That's all I have for now. Thank you." Bill pushed himself from the table and left the room.

Leaving the boardroom together, Frank whispered to the sales manager, Paul Grissom, "It sounds like Bill's got hold of a snake."

"Yeah," Paul responded. "I just hope he has hold of the right end."

"Eh. Bill's a tough guy. I don't think it matters to him which end he gets hold of."

"You're probably right, Frank." Paul walked down the hall toward his office. These were not the same accommodations he knew when he first started with Landover almost nine years ago. The recent renovations had brightened up the place and expanded some of the smaller offices—his being one of them. The carpet still had a faint remnant of its distinctive, new smell and the updated light fixtures and dropped ceilings everywhere gave the office area the look of a contemporary, professional organization. The lobby area had been dressed up with a new ceramic tile floor and expanded to make it more comfortable for visitors. The enlarged windows overlooking the front landscaping and parking lot brought in additional natural light and gave the lobby a more open feel. Just before he got to his office, Paul stopped to see Jack.

"Hey, Jack," he greeted him, as he stopped at Jack's doorway. Jack set his project folders aside and swiveled his office chair around to see his visitor.

"Good morning, Paul. What can I do for you?"

"I was just wondering if you had heard anything new regarding the Hartford Construction project."

"I'm thinking it's going to be a couple of months before they'll be ready to pull the trigger," Jack replied. "Dale said it's out of his hands until their board makes a decision, which may not be until after he retires."

"Dale's retiring?"

"He's just waiting on his HR department to put some final numbers together, which might be anywhere from three to four weeks, and when that's done, he's gone the next day."

"Good for him, but I hope this contract gets awarded before he retires. Hartford has been a great Landover customer over the years, and Dale has been a big part of that. We'll take all the help we can get on this project."

"I'm sure we're still in the hunt with Gantly, and I'm doing everything I can to keep our name fresh on Dale's mind. This 3.7-million-dollar deal is the largest I've ever worked on and worth every effort to bring it in."

"While I'm in here, you got any lunch plans today? I'm meeting Ben and Tony to try out that new place down the street and thought you might want to go along."

"Sorry, Paul, I just made an appointment with a new potential client."

"Great! Need anyone to tag along for moral support?"

"Probably not until I can get some more details. I don't want to run him off with a show of numbers, if you know what I mean."

"Understood. Maybe some other time. By the way, he's not an undercover IRS agent, is he? I'd hate to see you go to jail just over a lunch." Paul waved at Jack as he continued his way to his office.

"It never gets old, Paul," Jack said for Paul to hear. As he turned around to get back to his paperwork, he thought he heard a dull thud and stopped what he was doing to listen. After a few seconds of silence, he heard it again, this time a little louder, and sat motionless to detect the annoying sound's origin. Sensing it came from the direction of the hallway, he turned to test his theory and saw Jerry standing in his doorway. With a quick scan at the figure before him, he noticed Jerry's dress slacks were short of reaching his brown, suede-leather, safety shoes and his thin build made his short-sleeved shirt seem almost baggy. Jerry's black, horn-rim glasses reminded Jack of a 1960's documentary he had seen a few weeks earlier, and the simple, clip-on tie and pocket protector—pen, pencil and magic marker in place—seemed to bring it all together—geek. "Hey, Jerry, right?"

"Yes. I'm Jerry Simpson, the new safety director."

"I know! I recognized you from the new-employee orientation meeting last week. I'm Jack Fisher. Come on in and have a seat." Jack sat his folders on his desk and stood as Jerry approached him. Despite the invitation, Jerry remained standing.

"I really don't want to take up any of your time this morning," Jerry acknowledged, pushing his glasses up on his nose. "I'm still trying to meet everyone, and I know you're busy, but I just wanted to come by and introduce myself."

"Great! We're glad to have you on board."

"Thank you, Jack," Jerry said smiling, and then catching himself, "It is, Jack, isn't it?" he asked with a straight face.

"Yes, Jack Fisher."

"Sorry, I'm terrible with new names." Jerry dipped his head.

"That's alright; don't worry about it. You'll learn everyone's name soon enough."

"I sure hope so."

"Are you married, Jerry?"

"Oh, no. Not yet. I'm still waiting for Mrs. Right. You know: organized, smart, punctual, safety conscious, and, of course, someone who knows her way around an updated PC."

"Sounds like you've put a lot of thought into this and got her all spec'd out."

"Life is too short to assume you can find a woman like that just anytime or anywhere."

Or at all, Jack thought.

"That's why I decided a long time ago to not settle for anything less and start my search early."

"I'm sure there's a woman out there somewhere that possesses all those," *what are they?* "romantic qualities you're looking for." *Imagine, a female version of Jerry. The thought alone gives me goose bumps.*

"I know I've set my standards high, but I believe if I wait long enough, I'll find her. There have been a couple of close calls, but spreadsheets and databases were their ultimate weaknesses, and those are basic computing skills. Don't you agree?"

Jack was taken aback. *Computing skills, yes, but requirements for a spouse? Is he looking for a wife or a robot?* "Yeah, basic. Spreadsheets and data …bases. Very basic." Jack continued to nod his head. *I can see their wedding now: two people at the altar in safety attire, video games at the reception, and a gathering of every computer guru within a 300-mile radius for sci-fi charades.* "Hey, I just had an idea. Have you met Carl, the maintenance man?"

"I don't think I have."

"If you met him, you'd remember. He's a big burly man."

"Burly?" Jerry asked, his eyes widening.

"And he has a deep, gruff voice."

"Gruff?" Jerry swallowed. "He sounds aggressive."

"Oh no, not Carl. He's pretty easy going. I thought of him because he's single, too." Jerry gave Jack an awkward look. "No! I didn't mean that. Maybe you two could help each other. You see, Carl's also looking for a wife and finding one for him is going to be, uh, similar to your situation. You know—"

"Challenging?"

"Exactly! Challenging! At the very least, challenging. So maybe you two could counsel each other."

"You mean like give advice?"

"Give advice, listen, or share experiences."

"What would we talk about?"

"Whatever you like. Maybe one of your hunting trips."

"I've never been on one of those. Guns are too heavy for me, and my mother says the excessive recoil is not good for my tenuous shoulder. I shot a .22 rifle once and the pain from that told me she was right."

"How about fishing?"

"My dad took me fishing a lot when I was small. After I got my first rod and reel, I could never get the hang of setting the hook. The one time I did, a fish pulled my rod and reel into the lake, and I never saw it again. Just never had the desire for it since."

"Did you play Football in high school or college?"

"Too aggressive. I pulled a hamstring in high school, as assistant equipment manager, trying to carry too many football helmets at one time. Imagine if I had been on the team!"

"Are there any sports you like?"

"Not to participate in. My slender build and arrhythmic gate render me physically unable to be competitive in most sports; at least, that's how my high school coaches used to explain it. I don't mind watching."

"Then watch a game together while you discuss your female acquaintances."

"What if we don't have a female acquaintance yet?"

"You can talk about the kind of acquaintance you're looking for. Who knows, you may be able to find a wife for each other."

"But what if we become interested in the same woman?"

Jack tilted his head. "I'm not sure that's possible, Jerry. But if it happens, may the better man win." He slapped Jerry on the shoulder.

Jerry rubbed his shoulder as he gave thought to Jack's idea. "It could work."

"Oh, come to think of it, I believe Carl's still on vacation, which explains why you two haven't met yet, but he should be back next week."

"I look forward to meeting him. Now, Jack, are you in sales?"

"I'm one of three equipment salesmen we have here." Jerry nodded his head as he listened. "Have you met the other two,

Ben Reed and Tony Evans?"

"I met them last Wednesday when Paul was showing me around a little bit. Paul said he had another salesman, but he was out beating the bushes for more business. I guess that was you."

"Probably so. I try to keep things stirred up around here. In fact, I just received my first SOTY." Jack retrieved his coveted prize from its decorative display stand and showed it to Jerry.

"SOTY?" Jerry asked.

"Salesman of the Year; S-O-T-Y, SOTY," Jack enunciated.

"Oh. Is that a rock?" Jerry asked, as he gazed at the ornament.

"It's not just a rock," Jack responded.

"It looks like a rock, maybe polished quartz."

"This is a beautiful crystal, almost twice the size of a silver dollar, with gold leaf trim. Notice the gorgeous engraving." He handed the SOTY to Jerry, who gave it a quick look.

"Oh, yes, crystal. I should've known," he said, looking up at Jack and nudging his glasses with his nose. "I have a sister named Crystal." Jack was amused by the off-the-cuff comment, though he tried not to show it. "I guess I should go and let you get back to work." Jerry handed the SOTY back to Jack. "It was good to meet you, Jack. I'm sure we'll see each other around. Have a good day," as he gestured a wave by raising and lowering his right hand in a brisk, yet shy, fashion.

"You, too, Jerry, and it was good to meet you."

Jerry motioned to leave, but turned back, and pointed toward Jack's computer keyboard. "You might want to take a look at the wrist rest you're using for your keyboard. It doesn't appear to be high enough to fully relieve the pressure from your wrists while typing. Perhaps you should consider a more ergonomic option." Jerry gave Jack a visual demonstration using his own hands.

Jack turned his head, glanced down at his keyboard behind him, and looked back at Jerry. "Sure. I'll take a look at that, Jerry. Thanks."

"Alrighty, Jack. We don't want any carpal tunnel issues." Jerry

10

used his left hand to squeeze his right wrist and opened and closed his right hand several times as another demonstration. "I'll see you around." Jerry turned to leave Jack's office and just as he exited the doorway, he noticed something in the floor. He stooped down, pulled a small utility knife from his pants pocket, and used the miniature scissors to cut off an extra-long loop of snagged carpet fiber. Jerry stood to his feet, showed the remnant to Jack, and said with a serious tone, "This is no friend to high heels." Jack stood speechless as Jerry walked away.

"He is safety conscious, I'll give him that," Jack said.

Chapter 2

Across town, Charles Gantly, president of Gantly Industrial Sales, Landover's local competitor, arrived at 8:00am for his Friday-morning staff meeting. "Good morning, Mr. Gantly," Claire said, as he stepped into the lobby.

"Good morning, Claire," he said in his naturally rough voice. "Any messages?"

"None this morning," she replied.

"Thank you," he said, as he made his way down the hall, whistling as he walked.

Seated in the boardroom, "Here he comes," Ray said to Darryl, in a low voice.

"Yep," Darryl, agreed. "Everyone recognizes that heel-toe cadence." Darryl looked at Ray. "Long or short?" Ray held up one finger.

"Short," Ray answered.

"You're on," Darryl acknowledged.

Charles stepped into his office long enough to drop off his fedora and suit coat, then headed straight to the boardroom. He stopped at the door and gave a quick glance around the long, conference table. Ray and Darryl looked at his tie length. Darryl shook his head and slipped Ray a one-dollar bill. "Good morning, everyone," Charles announced.

"Good morning, Mr. Gantly," almost everyone replied.

Then, cupping his hands around his mouth, "Good morning, Jonathan," he directed toward the opposite end of the conference table, where Jonathan sat alone. Everyone laughed.

"Charles," Jonathan responded, lifting his fingers from the table for a lazy hand wave.

Noticing Ray folding his newly acquired one-dollar bill, "What was it today, fellas, my worn-out shoes or frayed tie?" Charles asked, as he closed the door and took his seat at the end of the table, setting his files in front of him.

"Frayed tie," Ray answered. "Actually, short, frayed tie." Charles looked down at his tie.

"Yeah, I gave up after three tries," he said. "I guess I should take better care of my suits, but they're just clothing. Anyone missing this morning?"

"Everyone's here but Lou, Mr. Gantly," answered Cliff. "He's still a little under the weather, but he should be back Monday or Tuesday."

"I'm glad to hear he's doing better," Charles said. "Pneumonia is nothing to play with. We'll miss not having a purchasing agent for a few days, but he needs to get better. Speaking of better, Cliff," he continued, while organizing his material, "that's a nice haircut."

"Yeah," Ray added. "Who's your barber? My guy died a couple of weeks ago and I need to find someone to cut my hair before I start looking like a hippie."

"What's wrong, Ray?" Darrell chided. "Your hair starting to touch your ears again?" A little light humor seemed to mellow things a bit. Even Jonathan managed to crack a smile.

"He's over on Eighteenth Street. His name is Bruno, and He's a retired construction worker," Cliff responded.

"Retired?" Ray asked.

"Yes, retired. But I don't think he's going to die on you anytime soon, if that's your concern; he's only forty-three."

"Must be a construction business I'm not familiar with to retire at that age," Charles quipped. "Let's get started." He retrieved his reading glasses from his shirt pocket, positioned them toward the end of his nose and thumbed through his papers until he found the Profit & Loss, or P&L, statement he was looking for. He glanced over the pages to refresh his memory, having reviewed the numbers the night before. Then laying the papers down, he peered over his reading glasses and said in a calm, stern voice, "As all of you are aware, our P&L statement is reflecting a very poor year-to-date performance, and, if we don't do something soon, this year could close at a substantial loss." He leaned back in his chair, removed his reading glasses, and laid them on the table. "We've had bad years before, but the economy is strong right now, so there's no excuse to lose money this year. I believe there are several factors that have gotten us to this point, but I also believe that any real solution is going to take a long time to achieve sustainable results. However, we've got to start thinking of ideas we can use now to generate a more immediate stream of revenue to tide us over while this long-term solution, whatever it may be, is implemented and develops into a more durable business model. Last week I asked a few of you to come up with some marketing ideas, things we can try to increase our business. I realize you haven't had much time, but I need you to present what you have to the group this morning for discussion. Without any further ado, let's just start at my left with Cliff and go around the table."

Cliff sat up, clasped his tie, and brushed his hand once down the length of it to be sure it was straight. "As you have pointed out, Mr. Gantly, our company does need a more immediate source of revenue to help us in the short term. Though the parts department has always performed consistently, we are eager to assist the other departments that have not been as fortunate. We also realize we cannot rely simply on past performance, but we must think outside the box and develop new opportunities. Now, I've—"

"Hold on, Cliff," Charles interrupted. "Let's not confuse consistently with positively. Parts sales have been consistent but have not been growing positively year-over-year for some time. In fact, parts sales have been relatively flat for several years." Cliff's pleasant facial expression seemed to melt away while most everyone else gave Charles a not-too-obvious stare of shock.

Jonathan sat with his side to the table, showing no concern for the proceedings, as if in his own little world, but he had to snicker at Cliff's chiding. *He couldn't manage a high school bake sale, let alone a parts department that must make real profits.*

Charles continued, "Since my father's passing, some twelve years ago, we have always presented ourselves as a sales-driven company, which has sustained us through some lean years, and our success has relied very little on parts revenue during this period. Times have changed to require a more balanced approach. I have come to realize my years of ignoring, rather than encouraging, the successful growth of other departments has put us at risk of losing market share. Consistent is great, but we must strive for consistent growth. I like your idea of thinking outside the box, and I didn't want to interrupt you, but thought I must make that distinction."

"Thank you, Mr. Gantly," Cliff responded in a more somber tone. His cheeks now glowing red, he sat silent for a moment before continuing. "I've done," he started in a squeaky voice. "Ahem. Excuse me." He took a quick drink from his water glass, while Ray and Darrell shared a comical smile. "I've done some quick analysis of our industry, and it appears that there are some charges we're not taking advantage of. For example, there are companies that have implemented environmental fees on every purchase, regardless of the gross value of the sale."

Why not charge them for the air they consume while they're waiting at the parts counter, Jonathan thought. *With your department's efficiency this could be a major revenue stream.*

"Some customers don't like paying them," Cliff continued, "but most believe it's necessary to help keep the environment clean. With the general populous in favor of clear blue skies and cleaner water, I can imagine there will be few, if any, complaints. If we were to start charging these fees on all parts purchases and not have any environmental issues throughout the year, the profits from the fees could simply go to the bottom line."

"Any comments on this from anyone," Charles asked the silent group. Cliff sat as though on pins and needles, darting his eyes around at the other attendees, but keeping his head still. After a short moment of thought, Ray spoke up.

"I have something, Mr. Gantly." Cliff forced a smile and eased his head and upper body toward Ray's direction. "It sounds like a good idea, Cliff, but programs like this can backfire. In my many years of service experience I've seen a lot of good customers come and go, often from failed programs put together to increase overall profits with no added value for the customer. For example, in the past we've tried to implement disposal fees on all replaced parts, regardless of their core value, to increase service revenue, but customers saw right through it and took their business elsewhere. I'm just saying, if we're going to do something like this, we need to be careful."

"Good point, Ray," Charles agreed, as Cliff straightened his body and stared down at his notepad in front of him. "Any other comments on this matter from anyone?" Again, Cliff sat motionless as he scanned the room. Everyone was silent. "I think we should move with this, but exercise caution as Ray has pointed out. It won't take long to start getting customer responses as to how it will be received." Cliff let out a silent exhale and lowered his shoulders as he closed his eyes for a second. Charles put on his reading glasses and scribbled a note on his pad. "Anything else, Cliff?"

Cliff offered a surprised look toward Charles. "No, sir. I'm still working on additional possibilities, but nothing substantial to add at this time."

Jonathan used his hand to hide his disgusted look from the others while pretending to rub his temple. *Nothing substantial to add; how he has succinctly described the value he brings to the company.*

"That was a good idea, Cliff. Continuing around the table, Ray, what have you got for us?"

"As long as I've been here, service has never been a big focus for us, as we all know. However, I would like to suggest that we try a promotional, designed specifically to generate additional service work. The program will be based on credits, or reward points, issued to customers who have work performed in our service shop or in the field. The number of points issued would be based on the type of work performed, whether a tune-up, overhaul, or whatever, and would accumulate over a calendar year. At any time during the year, when the points total allowed, they could be redeemed for free service work, or cash credit toward their unpaid ledger balance. I believe this will bring in additional service customers if they know they will eventually be getting something for free."

"I think that sounds like a good idea," Charles commented. "But we have to be sure the increase in service can be tracked and that the additional revenue generated from the program will more than offset the cost of what we give away." Charles turned to Jeffery. "Jeffery, you're the accountant. I didn't ask you to present anything this morning, but can we generate the data needed to monitor the impact of this program?"

"That will not be a problem if those responsible for service invoicing code the credits correctly. I can generate additional data fields in our reports for monitoring and train those responsible how to handle the credits."

"Very good, Jeffery. Thank you. Are there any comments from anyone else on the promotional?" Charles asked, as he jotted down some additional notes. Again, the room was silent, as everyone gave their approval of Ray's idea with a quick shake of their heads in response to his question. Jonathan sharply cut his eyes back toward the group to get an idea of consensus, though he was careful to not show any outward sign of concern. "Lisa, as Human Resources director, I'd like you to comment on our employee evaluations coming up in a couple of months. As everyone here is aware, if our revenue does not pick up and our business continues to slide, there will be no wage increases this year. Once that news gets out, I'm sure there will be several employees who will beat a path to your door."

"I'm aware of the potential, Mr. Gantly, and I think we are prepared to handle whatever comes up. Hopefully, most will not react negatively to the news, should it happen. For those that do, we will deal with on a case-by-case basis and try to retain our best people. For the short term that's about all we can do."

Jonathan turned his head to see Lisa's emotionless expression as she laid out her action plan. *My kind of manager: unabashed and to the point.*

"We certainly don't want to lose anyone," she continued, "but we're not exactly the best performing company out there right now, and most of our technicians would not have to look hard to find a job elsewhere should they decide to leave. We need to be thinking of a backup plan and things we can do for our employees if there are no raises; you know, morale boosters, things like that."

"We'll need to keep that in mind," Charles responded, as he made notes and continued around the table. "Darrell, is there anything new to add from the production side of things?"

"In the seven years I've been at Gantly, I would say our backlog is as low as I've ever seen it. We're not exactly to the point of laying people off, but we could be in four to six months if things don't pick up. We've already started cutting costs wherever we can, and we're working overtime only to get out really late or high-profile orders. We've also brought back in-house some of the weldment work we were having done through outside suppliers, which is helping to keep our welders busy, but it's not doing much for our mechanics. Honestly, Mr. Gantly, short of doing what I can to reduce internal costs and juggling my technicians to keep them productive, I don't know what else I can do. Ray and I have been discussing with Franklin the possibility of providing some of the after-sale services our customers now have performed at accessorizing companies to add options and special features that we don't currently offer, but that will require engineering time."

"Engineering, huh," Charles said, with a little disdain. "Gone are the days when the only bottle neck to making a sale was getting the paperwork processed." He jotted down a few notes. "It sounds like you're doing what you can, Darrell. Just keep plugging away at it." Then looking toward Franklin, "Franklin, I guess that's the perfect segue to you. I know this is your first attendance in one of our staff meetings, but I wanted to be sure to cover all the bases. Is there anything on the Engineering horizon regarding extra features or options we can add to our machines, soon?"

"We believe so, Mr. Gantly," Franklin began. "We, that is, Ray and I, and Darrell, too, we've been looking at a few things that we believe we could offer on some of our machines." He rubbed his sweaty palms over his upper thighs trying to use his jeans to keep his hands dry.

Thankfully, he's a better engineer than he is an orator, Jonathan thought, with a slight smile and shake of the head.

"Some of them," Franklin continued, "the options, are simple things, but that's really what most customers, that is, our cust...most of our customers are having added anyway. Not everything they're having added is simple, but most of what they're having added is." Ray gave Darrell a slight head gesture in Franklin's direction.

"Most of these added features," Darrell interjected, "are really simple concepts but we don't have many fully designed yet for our equipment." Franklin leaned back in his chair, tilted his head backward and took a few, slow, deep breaths, still rubbing his palms, no doubt thankful for Darrell's rescue from the clumsy conversational hole he was digging. "For example, on our larger machines, some customers like to install louvered guards to protect the engine radiator from road and construction debris, more so than the standard, factory guard that is presently offered. Franklin has designed a workable concept for one of our more popular models, the LX927, but we still need to fabricate a prototype and install it for testing to be sure radiator airflow is not overly obstructed."

"Are we not able to get any help from Billston?" Charles asked. "After all, it's their machines we're distributing."

"Billston provides minimal options from the factory, as you know," Darrell added, "though they do offer help to their distributors with the design and application of added features. Franklin is working with them on this new guard, and they've been extremely helpful."

"So, there is something in the works, right?" Charles asked.

"Yes, sir," Franklin responded, still fidgeting but not seeming quite as uncomfortable as before. "We want to be sure the options we design that they …they need to be easy to install for our shop guys 'cause that saves time, assembly time. I mean, if that option is added, it saves assembly time, right Darrell?"

"That's correct. Making them easy to install will save time."

"Also," Franklin added, now a little more confident, "the options, that is, the parts for the options, or add-ons, if you will, need to be designed so the assembly is the same every time, so no shop modifications will be necessary. And most importantly, actually, two very important things to consider are being sure the accessory doesn't interfere with the machine's ability to work, or, you know, to do its job correctly, and the liability we assume by installing the accessory." Franklin managed a slow exhale as he sat back in his chair and relaxed his upper body.

Finally! Jonathan thought. *The king of fragmented sentences has concluded.*

"Let's keep after this," Charles said. "If there are things we can do to enhance our equipment, we need to find ways to get them done. Every option we add is an opportunity to increase profits for our new equipment sales, and each of these options generates additional parts sales when replacements are required." Charles jotted down some additional notes. "I realize Lou's not in today, but I know he's been doing what he can to negotiate the best deals with respective suppliers to help reduce our costs and working with them to schedule our component deliveries on a timely basis. There's not much else we can expect from him." Charles looked toward the opposite end of the table, where Jonathan was glancing at his watch. "Jonathan, you're up next, or last, I should say, just as you prefer. As sales manager, tell us what we can do to increase sales!"

Jonathan turned his head toward the table when he heard his name, annoyed by the invitation to join them. *I simply must find a way to avoid these dreadful staff meetings. Nonetheless, let's see what kind of babble we can put together to pacify the crowd.* He spun his chair around to face the others, careful not to scuff his fine, Italian-leather shoes. He pulled on his gold cuff links to straighten his shirt-sleeve monograms, gleaned the time from his diamond-lined Rolex, and clasped his hands together as he laid them on the table. Only three years younger than Charles, his platinum-colored hair did not hide his age, though it created a nice blend with his gray suit. "I've listened intently to all that has been suggested," he started. Ray and Darrell exchanged surprised looks. "I feel that the ideas put forth so far will help generate additional revenue, albeit on a small scale. However, we must admit that sales have got to increase for us to realize any substantial gains." Jonathan stood up and made his way to the flip chart, where he had prepared some hand-drawn graphics. "As you can see on this first graph," he pointed out, "the value of medium-sized construction equipment sales in our area made by all suppliers combined has not decreased noticeably in the last four years but has maintained a fairly consistent level, around 125 million dollars annually." Then flipping to the next graphic, "But, as you can see on this chart, we have seen a steady decline in market share percentage over the last eighteen months. Two years ago, we had captured thirteen percent of the market, and now we find ourselves just under ten percent today. It is obvious we are losing our share in the marketplace to our competition. We have lost a little over three percent so far, or roughly 3.7 million dollars' worth on an annualized basis, and presently we are on a negative trend. This is the problem we need to fix." Jonathan could see he now had everyone's undivided attention. "For us to tackle this problem and succeed, we are all going to have to take some drastic measures and be willing to make some personal sacrifices."

"But Jonathan," Charles interrupted, "it's your group that needs to make the difference. What drastic measures can the other departments offer for additional equipment sales?"

Jonathan made eye-to-eye contact with Charles, looked in the direction of Lisa and Jeffery, who were not paying attention, and then motioned with a slight head movement toward the door.

"Uh, Lisa, Jeffery," then at the last moment, "Franklin," Charles said. They raised their heads and looked at each other when they heard their names, like kids caught with their hands in the cookie jar. "I guess you three really don't need to stay for the entire meeting, since your departments are not directly responsible for generating revenue. Please, go ahead and get back to what you were doing." The three stood without hesitation, gathered their things, and left the room, stranding Ray, Cliff, and Darrell, who stared in disbelief, following them with their eyes all the way out the door. Once they had exited, Charles set his reading glasses on the table, sat back in his chair, and looked at Jonathan. "Now, tell us what kind of drastic measures you're referring to."

Ray and Darrell exchanged curious glances while Cliff made annoying facial expressions as he tried to dislodge something from between his teeth. Darrell stared at Cliff as he pushed the toothpick holder over to him, which he graciously accepted. He extracted the malicious offender, chewed it a little more, and then swallowed.

"First of all," Jonathan said, as he leaned over the end of the table, supporting himself with both hands on the tabletop, "I must admit you are correct, Charles. It is my group that must make the most drastic changes. We must change the way we sell and close business, but I need the cooperation from everyone at this table. I need to know I can count on each of you to do whatever is necessary to generate revenue. Can I count on you?" he asked, as he looked each man in the eyes.

"Jonathan," Ray started, "you know each of us will do whatever we can to support the company, as we have already demonstrated in years past. But I'm not sure what kind of things you are referring to as being necessary."

"Gentlemen," Charles interjected, as he leaned over the table and made eye-to-eye contact with each of them, "my father started this company forty years ago, and I'm not about to see it fall apart on my watch. We will do what it takes to turn a profit. Based on the numbers Jonathan has presented, that three-percent loss in the marketplace translates to more than twenty percent of our annual sales. If we lose another two-to-three percent market share this company will most likely have to consider downsizing, possibly a sizeable portion of it. I hope that makes it very clear to each of you."

"Oh, sure, Mr. Gantly," Cliff answered. "Right, Ray, Darrell?"

"Sure, Mr. Gantly, I understand the consequences of our inaction," Ray admitted. Then, looking to Jonathan, "But I'd like to hear what it is you expect from us. How can we help?"

"We have to give our customers reasons to buy from us," Jonathan said. "Cliff, you mentioned additional fees you can charge your parts customers. What if we waive those fees to specific customers who are considering equipment purchase contracts, and to those who have made large equipment purchases in the last three months?" Jonathan was gesturing with his hands as he talked, while Charles squinted his eyes and turned his good ear toward Jonathan, as if he were asking him to repeat himself.

"That would show favoritism," Cliff responded, "and the

customers we do charge won't appreciate that."

Jonathan offered a quick smile. "I assure you that the financial benefits of an equipment purchase will far outweigh any grumblings and complaints you'll get from a few unhappy parts customers," he said. "Besides, it will take a while before anyone finds out who's paying the extra fees and who isn't. You will need to instruct each of your staff to keep it hush-hush, maybe to the point of threatening their job," he said without missing a beat. Charles closed his eyes, in an apparent attempt, though unsuccessful, to dismiss himself from the room.

"Whoa, Jonathan!" Ray interrupted. "You can't just threaten someone's job like that."

"Oh," Jonathan said. "Perhaps it was a poor choice of words on my part. I am simply saying that Cliff's staff will need to be compliant and submissive to his leadership, as their supervisor. Should they choose to divulge privileged information without first gaining permission they could be disciplined, up to and including termination. Does that sound better?" Jonathan asked, trying to hide his sarcasm. *So far, so good*.

"Go on," Ray responded.

"In regard to the program you suggested, Ray, what if we offered double or even triple points to customers who are considering an equipment purchase, and the credits become immediately available at the signing of the purchase contract? We could expand the program for these perspective customers to also include free service on personal vehicles for their respective purchasing agents. I believe this would go a long way to demonstrate our pricing flexibility to our customers." *That should certainly rile the troops*, Jonathan thought. *With that dropped jaw, Ray looks like a PEZ dispenser*.

Ray and Cliff looked at each other with astonishment. Finally, Ray found himself asking, "Is this legal?"

"I'll be honest with you, Ray," Jonathan replied, "it walks awfully close to the line but, yes, it is legal. Look," he pleaded, "I am trying to give us the best opportunity to make these programs work. You gentlemen have suggested them; I'm simply proposing a few, minor modifications to make them more marketable to the industry we serve and accessible to a greater mass of clientele." The room was silent for a moment while they all caught up with the double talk.

"Suppose we're all on board with what you're proposing, Jonathan," Ray offered. "Surely these programs are not going to work by themselves to entice a customer to spend hundreds-of-thousands of dollars with us just because they can get a free maintenance inspection or save a few bucks by not paying environmental fees on their parts. What's the real catch?"

"Catch?" Jonathan asked. "There is no catch. I am simply asking for your support in implementing these ideas with the refinements we have discussed. As far as getting any contracts inked, leave that to me and my staff." He had to laugh inside. *They must think I've gone mad. Their frantic looks say it all.*

"Gentlemen," Charles interrupted, "there appears to be a lack of agreement as to how these new proposals should ultimately interface with sales."

Absolutely, Jonathan thought. *Let Sales take care of Sales and leave these petty programs for others to waste time on.*

"For now, let's concentrate on the original ideas as something to start with. Let's put these in place immediately and monitor their progress. Maybe at some point, after we've consulted HR …and Legal, we can look at rolling in Jonathan's suggestions, or at least part of them. As has been discussed, Jonathan, these things are not going to work on their own. We are still going to need some major contracts from your group."

"I'm working on that, Charles, even as we speak."

Charles put his reading glasses back on and glanced over his notes and then addressed the other men. "Ray, I'll need you to work up a service flyer to advertise your new bonus plan and put copies in the service and parts departments. You might even try a mass mailing to all existing service customers. Cliff, as you have pointed out, environmental fees are becoming the norm. I say we implement these charges without any advertising or fanfare and see how they go. I'm sure there will be complaints, but your group can address them on a case-by-case basis. Put together some kind of plan or script, if you will, so all parts personnel will deal with these situations in the same manner. Does anyone have any questions?" The room was quiet. "Thank you, everyone, for your support."

The meeting was over, and most left the room as soon as they had gathered their things. Cliff and Ray sat for a moment trying to take in everything that they had just witnessed. "What do you think Jonathan's up to?" Ray asked.

"Who knows? Let's just hope Charles doesn't decide to go along with any of his harebrained ideas or we'll both have a lot of customer relations to mend. By the way, the bonus plan was a good idea you had." They stood up and pushed in their chairs. "Where did you get that from?"

"It worked at my dad's auto repair center in Houston, so I thought it might work in our business here." Ray followed Cliff to the door. "Where did you get your idea?"

"Oh, you'd be surprised how many ideas go through your mind when you're sitting on the cutting edge." Ray offered a bewildered look as Cliff walked away.

Chapter 3

Once the meeting was over, Jonathan made his way to Tom Brandent's office and stuck his head in the door. "Tom, do you have a moment?"

"Sure, Jonathan, come on in," Tom replied, as he finished writing a note. When he saw Jonathan reach for the door, time seemed to enter a new, slower dimension. Every sound was so distinct: the jingle of the knob when Jonathan grabbed it, the squeak of the hinges as the door rotated about its pins, the diminishing noise from the hallway as the door opening grew smaller, the ping of the latch when it hit the strike plate, even the sound of the latch as it was forced against the spring in the receiver, the click of the latch as it cleared the hole in the strike plate, and, finally, the dull thud of the door landing against the semi-cushioned jamb. It was done. The door was closed. His spirit sank within him, and he rolled his eyes as Jonathan took a seat in front of his desk. *Oh no! Here we go again,* he thought.

"Tom," Jonathan began in a very relaxed tone, "I'll make this short and sweet."

Short and sweet, Tom thought. *The only thing that would make this sweet is for the conversation to be shorter than it already has been. Forgive me, Lord. Please help me hear him out.*

"As you are aware," he began, "we are losing market share faster than we can write the checks to cover our losses. Our job as sales is to stop this cycle and turn things around. To do this, it will require every salesman going the extra mile to see that we close our business in a timely manner and that we close all the business we get involved with. From you, Tom, I am expecting at least a thirty-five-percent close ratio."

A thirty-five-percent close ratio? Is he crazy? Tom thought. "Jonathan, I'm not sure how you expect me to achieve that. Nothing close to those numbers has been achieved by anyone in this industry that I am aware of. You know I've never shied away from working late hours or even days off to increase business, but even that won't get thirty-five percent. Besides, the customer makes the final decision, and I can't change that."

"Tom," Jonathan said in a calm voice, "you must get more creative in your sales technique. You can't submit your bid and just sit on your hands waiting for someone to decide between you and your competition. You've got to go into action! Provide some motivational stimulant. Think about it," he said, leaning forward. "What says, 'Pick me!' to a purchasing agent more than a big-screen television, or a ski trip to Colorado?"

Tom paused for a moment. *Surely, he didn't just say that.* "Are you telling me to bribe customers to get their business?"

"Bribe is a very strong word, Tom," Jonathan answered, as he sat back in his chair and brushed his hands along his suit sleeves. "I'm sure that's not what you meant to say. I am simply suggesting that you reward your customers prematurely for their perspective purchase or for graciously accepting your bid proposal. Does that sound better?"

"Jonathan, no matter how you twist the words, it's still a bribe, and I don't do business that way."

"When business changes, you must alter your approach to secure that business," Jonathan said, as he sat up.

"I can alter my approach without resorting to shifty tactics," Tom retorted.

"These tactics you characterize as shifty have been employed by some of the more financially successful salesmen of our era; people who willfully changed to become what they wanted to be. You needn't blight their triumphs with your petty morals!"

"Petty they may seem to you, Jonathan, but they're what I choose to help govern my life."

Jonathan leaned over Tom's desk and pointed his finger at him. "Look, Tom," he said with a very stern voice, and getting progressively louder, "either you get on board, or you can get out! We currently have a 3.7-million-dollar perspective order hanging out there, and if you can't bring it in, it will be your last chance with me!"

Tom bit his tongue, knowing he could not afford to say what was on his mind, nor did he really want to. He prayed back carnal thoughts that used to easily manipulate his speech and actions as he formulated his response. "Jonathan, I know you're under a lot of pressure to turn things around, but this isn't helping. I'll do my best."

"I'm not asking you to do your best! I'm telling you to bring in this contract! Got It?" he barked, as he slammed his fist on Tom's desk and stood up to leave. "This is a man's world, Tom! You need to step up and do a man's job! If you aren't talented enough to compete in the equipment business on a high level then pack your things and go sell something more fitting to your puritan ways, like handmade cookware or candle lanterns."

Cookware? Lanterns? Is he serious? I can feel my empathy for him starting to wane. "Jonathan, I'm doing everything I can to bring in business, but you're making it very difficult. Sometimes I feel like I want to—"

"Quit?" Jonathan interjected. "The day you decide to throw in the towel don't worry about sticking around here. I need men who aren't afraid of making challenging decisions or implementing innovative solutions. When the time comes you can't follow my lead, submit your resignation and seek a new vocation!" He stomped to the door and, before opening it, turned back at Tom and said, "When this contract is awarded, it better be for Gantly equipment!" He grabbed the handle, jerked the door open, without allowing it to hit the wall, and stormed out.

Tom sat dumbfounded. "I was going to say scream," he snickered, "but quit will work, too. And to think, after lunch, I was going to share my candy bar with him." He threw himself back, into his chair, closed his eyes, and swiveled his chair back and forth. *When a grown man, my supervisor, throws a tantrum in my office it's time for something to change.*

Jonathan took a moment in the hallway to straighten his tie and gather his wits before walking toward his office. "That man really gets under my skin," he muttered, as he pulled his monogrammed handkerchief from his coat pocket and wiped it across his mouth. "Someday, that little goody two-shoes is going to learn how to play by my rules, and then he'll thank me for my insightful motivation."

"Jonathan!" Charles called out, just before Jonathan walked into his office. As Charles approached, he offered a bewildering stare. "Are you okay?" he asked. "Your cheeks look a little rosy."

"I'm fine, Charles. Just a little excited about our positive potential."

"On that note, if you've got time, I'd like to go to lunch with you and discuss the sales strategy you're working on."

"I can't, today, but if you have a few moments, I believe I can give you a preliminary rundown."

"Sure," Charles responded, as they both stepped into Jonathan's office.

His office was spacious and accommodating. A large oak desk positioned in just the right location to take advantage of the window views, surrounded by comfortable leather chairs for his guests, which matched his larger, palatial office chair. A medium-sized table set off to one side offered space for customer presentations and departmental meetings. Pictures of Jonathan with several of his customers at various events were hung on the wall. Like most salesmen, Jonathan enjoyed golf and his office displayed many such mementos. "Please, have a seat, Charles," Jonathan offered, as he took his seat behind his desk. "As we are aware, our market share is not what it was, or what it could be. We've grown accustomed to expecting above thirteen percent and now find ourselves struggling to reach ten. Charles, you and I agree that it is Sales that makes things happen, and I'm working on a project, which I believe will give us significant results."

"Good, good," he said, nodding his head. "Let's hear it."

"I believe we can turn things around in a relatively short time. In fact," he said, as he leaned forward, "I believe we can be back to where we were in as little as eight to ten months."

"Do you mean back to our previous market-share level?" he asked, as he rubbed his hands together.

"I believe the difference will be indistinguishable. In addition, our market share will have the potential to grow year-over-year as customers grow attuned to our mutually complimentary growth strategy."

"Mutually complimentary?"

"The customer receives a quality product in exchange for full payment, which we gladly accept into our corporate coffer and use to reward the salesman who was able to use his talent and budgeted resources to acquire the business. Mutually complimentary." Charles stared through Jonathan, as he tried to make sense of what he just heard. "Who knows?" he continued. "In two or three years we could break the fifteen-percent barrier!" Charles awoke from his numbness.

"Fifteen percent? Are you sure about this? I mean, Jonathan, you've done some remarkable things in the past, but this would certainly outdo them all. Tell me how you plan to do this." Jonathan could sense he had touched a receptive nerve with Charles—his money nerve.

"Right now, I am in the middle of some very sensitive negotiations with a potential team member that, when settled, will make some astonishing transformations in this business, and at Gantly. I regrettably refrain from going into any details with you at the moment, Charles, and respectfully ask that you trust me on this. I would never do anything to compromise the company, and I believe you know that."

"But what's with all the secrecy?"

"I'm just trying to be respectful to the other party involved. I don't want to precipitate any rumors that may jeopardize one's current employment or reputation in their respective industry."

Charles sat back in his chair, mulling his options. "I feel like I'm kind of sticking my neck out a little here for you, Jonathan. I know you always do things with the best interest of the company in mind. Tell me how much time you need."

"Give me a couple of weeks," Jonathan responded, as he leaned back in his chair, "and I should be ready to present my entire plan."

Charles thought about it for a moment. "Okay, Jonathan, two weeks it is." He stood to his feet and playfully wagged his finger at Jonathan as he said with a smile, "We're all counting on you, and I know you can do it."

"Thank you, Charles." As Charles left his office, Jonathan folded his hands behind his head, satisfied with his performance. "When this is all over, Charles will probably put me in charge of the entire company while he retires to the Bahamas."

Meanwhile, Alan Beckett, owner of Beckett Construction, had been notified earlier in the morning that his DL385XP was repaired and ready for pickup at the Landover service department. He pulled his trailer through the main service entrance with his half-ton dually and parked in a convenient loading area. He stepped out of his truck, stomped his boots on the pavement a few times to dislodge any dried mud, pressed his cowboy hat firmly over his wavy, black hair, and made his way to the front service desk, where he met Tim, one of the service writers.

"May I help you, sir?"

"Yesser. I'm Alan Beckett with Beckett Construction," he said, brushing his hand over his short, neatly trimmed beard, "and we dropped off a DL385XP yesterd'y to get it fixed and somebody called me to let me know it was ready fer pick up."

"Give me just a moment, sir, while I check on it." Tim flipped through his job folders and came across the one for Beckett Construction. "Here it is." Tim pulled the folder and opened it to review the service report. "Let's see. Yes, it is complete. The total bill is $283.67." Tim pulled a copy of the invoice from the folder and handed it to Mr. Beckett. Pointing down the hall, he said "You can take that to the cashier for payment, and then we'll get you loaded."

"What was wrong with it?" he asked, looking at his invoice.

Tim opened the folder once again to look over the paperwork. "It looks like it just needed a little maintenance," he replied, giving Mr. Beckett a short summation of the report. "The original filters were still on the package and the engine has over six-hundred hours runtime. That's a lot over the limit of typical recommended filter and oil changes."

Mr. Beckett paused for a moment and then commented, "But'chu guys are responsible fer all the filter changes fer the first six munts."

"Oh, no sir, Mr. Beckett," Tim explained. "It has always been our policy, as it is with any supplier, that consumables such as filters, belts, hoses, and the like are the responsibility of the customer. These type items are part of the standard, routine maintenance program for the equipment and are not considered warranty issues. I'm afraid you'll have to pay for this one."

"But I'm sure it's part o' my contract," Mr. Beckett countered. "I most cert'nly remember askin' about this before I bought the tractor. Just ask the fella that sold it to me."

"Do you have a copy of the contract with you, Mr. Beckett?"

"I thank I do." He tilted his head. "Where did I last see that thang? I'll go look in my truck and see if I can find it. Maybe it's in my briefcase. I'll be right back."

As Mr. Beckett walked out into the parking lot, Tim called Steven Baker, the service manager. "Service. This is Steven. How may I help you?"

"Steven, Mr. Beckett, with Beckett Construction, is here to pick up his DL385XP that needed a total filter change, and he says it's part of his contract for us to provide free filter changes for the first six months. I tried to tell him that's not customary with any supplier, but he insists that it applies to this piece of equipment. He's on his way to his truck to see if he has a copy of his contract with him. What should I do?"

"How much money are we talking about?"

"$283.67."

"And the filters were the only problem?"

"That's correct."

"If he finds his contract, and the special conditions mention the filter changes, we must honor that. If he can't find his contract, then we'll pull a copy of it here and review it. In fact, while he's looking in his truck, I'm going to go ahead and pull a copy of it now. I'll bring it down when I find it."

Tim hung up the phone and waited for Mr. Beckett to return while Steven searched their database for an electronic copy of the contract. In short order, Steven found the contract, glanced it over for any special conditions, printed it out, and headed for the front service desk. Steven arrived about the same time Mr. Beckett came walking back in with his purchase contract in his hand.

"I knew I had it somewherr," Mr. Beckett said, as he approached Tim at the service desk. He showed the contract to Tim and pointed at the special-conditions clause. "Right here it says Landover will cover filter changes fer the first six munts."

"Hi, Mr. Beckett," Steven interrupted. "I'm Steven Baker, the service manager."

"Glad to meet'cha, Mr. Baker."

"The pleasure's all mine, Mr. Beckett. Tim tells me you have a contract with some special provisions, and I was wondering if I may be able to look at it. We want to be sure we provide you with all the services you've been promised."

"Sure," Mr. Beckett said, and handed it over to Steven. Steven read the special provisions of the contract, and they were listed just as Mr. Beckett had stated.

"May I make a copy of this contract, Mr. Beckett, so we'll have it on file for you next time?"

"Go right ahead. It don't matter t' me." Steven walked over to the service desk to make a copy and Tim followed him, leaving Mr. Beckett alone.

"We can't argue with a contract," Steven said. "Write the job up as a no-cost work order and policy all the labor and material. Print Mr. Beckett a new invoice showing no charge for this work and then help him get his equipment loaded so he can be on his way. I'll file this copy for future reference." Then returning to Mr. Beckett, Steven handed him the original contract. "We're sorry for the confusion, Mr. Beckett. It appears we didn't have a copy of your latest contract on file, which would have alerted us about the special provisions. Tim will print you a new copy of your invoice to show no charge for this service work, and help you get your equipment loaded. We appreciate your business. Please come again."

"I 'preciate it, Mr. Baker. Thank you," he said, as he made his way back out to his truck to wait for his equipment.

"His contract actually says that?" Tim asked.

"His contract actually says that," Steven said, as he watched Mr. Beckett walk out. Tim printed out the new invoice and followed Mr. Beckett outside to help load his equipment. Steven turned around and started back to his office, "But our copy of the contract does not say that," he muttered.

"Hey, Steven," Jerry called from down the hall, smiling as he came closer.

Steven stopped as Jerry approached him. "Oh, hi, Jerry. How's it going?" Steven noticed something odd about Jerry's face and stared at him as he came nearer.

"It's going pretty good, so far, Steven," Jerry said at a slowing pace before finally pausing. "Is there something wrong?" he asked, staring back at Steven.

Steven could not help but notice Jerry was wearing safety goggles over his regular eyeglasses. Not just any goggles, but large, laboratory goggles. But they had to be large to fit over his horn-rim glasses. "I didn't know we had a chemical lab here," Steven remarked.

"What do you mean?" Jerry asked. "Oh, the goggles," he said with a sudden awakening, as he reached to remove them. "They're so comfortable I always forget I have them on."

"Comfortable?" Steven asked.

"I've adjusted the elastic band to provide just the right amount of cerebral pressure for a soothing sensation that helps me relax."

"Extra cerebral pressure is the last thing I need right now," Steven said. "Making your rounds?"

"I was just showing myself around, trying to get more familiar with the facility. All the various departments seem to fit together nicely regarding overall efficiency."

"It wasn't always like this. As I'm sure you're aware, we just recently completed some major renovations that took us over three years. Most of our departments had grown so much over the years that they seemingly became scattered all over the property and needed to be consolidated. I've been with Landover for over twenty years and these new renovations make me feel like I'm working at a brand-new company. We're all excited about it."

"They certainly do look nice."

"So, what's going on, today, in the world of safety?"

"I'm making a few preliminary Personal-Protective-Equipment inspections, or PPE inspections as we safety guys call them. You know, walking around the different areas to be sure everyone is wearing the proper attire for their respective area: safety glasses, steel-toe shoes, and the like. I'm trying to get a feel for everyone's acceptance of the safety program. So far, it appears most don't have to be reminded to put on their safety glasses, which is a usual weak link for most companies with safety policies."

"We try to heavily emphasize safety in all our work areas, especially in the service shop and the production area. Our last safety director was a stickler for safety, too."

"It looks like he did a very good job of instilling the importance of safety in most everyone here."

"I'm sure you'll pick up right where he left off."

"I'll certainly do my best," he replied, almost embarrassed by the kind words. "I better get going. I'm having lunch today with the production manager, Glen Adams, but I'll see you around."

"Alright, Jerry. Enjoy your lunch." Steven smiled as he continued his walk back to his office. "Got to love these safety guys."

Chapter 4

Mr. Edwards arrived at the restaurant right on time. Rather than circle through the parking lot looking for a place to park, he pulled up to the front drive, exited his vehicle, and was met by the valet. "Do you have driving gloves?" Mr. Edwards asked.

"Driving gloves?" the attendant questioned.

"Never mind," he said, as he surveyed the young man's uniform and handed him his keys. "Careful with the carpet. I just had it cleaned."

"Yes, sir."

"Young man," he said, as the valet clicked his seatbelt, "I know everything about my vehicles."

"Yes, sir," he replied, as he closed the door and screeched off to find a parking spot.

Mr. Edwards shook his head. "I guess I should be thankful he was wearing shoes." He brushed off his suit, checked his hair, and straightened his tie before walking inside.

The restaurant was a better-than-average dining establishment that specialized in steak and seafood. The menu did not include any unusual selections, but everything seemed to always be cooked to perfection. Its walls were lined with autographed pictures of some of its well-known dining guests, including many local dignitaries. Mirrors were strategically placed around the dining room to give it a much more open atmosphere, yet many of the booths still provided a sense of privacy, perfect for a romantic evening or an informal business meeting.

"Welcome to McCardy's," the lady at the hostess station said. "How many in your party?"

"I'm here to meet another gentleman, Mr. Jack Fisher."

"One moment please, while I check the register." After a short pause, "Mr. Fisher is at table twenty-four. If you'll wait just one moment, I'll have someone show you to the table." In just a few seconds she had summoned a waitress close by, who gladly escorted him to the dining area.

"This way, please," she directed, as she led him through the maze of tables and chairs. The typical lunch crowd kept the place packed, and today was no exception. Most came for the excellent food, as the aroma of the blackened seafood and grilled steaks excited even the laziest of palates. His personal favorite was the grilled salmon with seasonal veggies, which already had his mouth salivating.

Table twenty-four was situated in a nice, quiet area of the restaurant. Jack had met several clients here before, and he knew where the best tables were to discuss business with the least interruptions. The music was mellow, easy-listening style, played just loud enough to qualify as background noise when no one was talking, should that ever occur.

Upon arriving at the table, "Here we are," the waitress said. "Your server will be right with you."

"Thank you," he said, as she walked away. As Jack stood to greet his guest, his happy look transformed to a leery stare at the somewhat familiar figure.

"Mr. Edwards?" he said.

"Mr. Fisher," he replied as the two shook hands.

"It's a pleasure to meet you," Jack said, as a million thoughts raced through his mind while he digested their introduction.

"Oh, the pleasure is all mine, Mr. Fisher. Please, let's sit down." Mr. Edwards took his seat, as Jack hesitated then drifted into his seat, never taking his eyes off him. The light over the table granted a more revealing image.

I know I've seen this guy before; but where? Jack thought. Mr. Edwards picked up his menu from the table and began to peruse the selections.

"The grilled salmon is always so good here," he commented without lifting his eyes from his menu. "But I guess I should check out the specials before I make my final decision."

While staring at the back of Mr. Edward's menu, Jack's mind was on overload, trying to pull an identity from his mental database to match his new, potential client. After a few moments of unsuccessful retrievals, the stars seemed to align and the pieces fell into place, as he now recognized his guest. "Mr. Edwards," Jack said in a monotone voice.

"Yes, Mr. Fisher," he replied, in a relaxed mode, still perusing his menu. Then, noticing the special, "Oh look, blackened tilapia. I wonder if it comes with brown rice."

"Mr. Edwards, I know who you are."

"I know who I am, too, Mr. Fisher," he acknowledged, after dipping his menu to show his face, then raising it again.

"I know who you are, and it's not going to work. I recognize you from a magazine article I read. You're Jonathan Edwards, the sales manager for Gantly!"

"Right, again, Mr. Fisher."

"You're not going to get any competitive information from me. I'm not your average, naïve, young, unsuspecting salesman."

Jonathan laid his menu down to look Jack in the face. "Oh, I know exactly who you are, Jack." Jonathan, again, raised his menu, as Jack got a deep, sinking feeling that somebody was being played. As Jack sat spellbound, staring at the back of Jonathan's menu, with his jaw dropped, the waitress came to the table.

"Hello, gentlemen, my name is Myra and I'll be your server

this afternoon. What can I get you two to drink?"

"I believe I'll have a glass of tea with lemon," Jonathan offered.

"And for you, sir?" she directed to Jack.

Still mystified, Jack managed the awareness to roll his head toward Myra and answered, "Tea… I'll have tea." *Something's not right about this situation*, he thought as he stared at Myra. *Can you help me understand this?*

"Are you gentlemen ready to order, or do you need a couple of minutes?"

"Oh, I'm sure I know what I want," Jonathan said. "How about you, Jack?" Jonathan asked, gesturing his hand in Jack's direction.

As the question was asked, Jack turned his head back in the direction of Jonathan and stammered, "Uh, I …, sure, I'm ready." Moving a little more fluid, he turned back to Myra and rattled off, "I'll have the eight-ounce T-bone, cooked medium-well and a baked potato."

"And the dressing for your salad?" She asked.

"R …an …ch," he enunciated with all the diction he could muster. Myra retrieved his menu while he continued his stare. *I wonder if she can read my mind and realize how bad I need to get out of here.*

"And for you, sir?" she asked Jonathan. Jack turned to hear his response.

"I'll have the grilled salmon and seasonal veggies," and handed her his menu. Then turning to Jack, he added, "It's my favorite, though I almost went for the blackened tilapia." Jack offered a half-smile.

"Thank you," she said, as she gathered the menus. "I'll have this right out."

When she left the table, Jack watched as she slipped away, and felt abandoned, alone with a total stranger. *Couldn't she have stayed just a moment longer? Where is Paul? I need to get out of this trap. No cheese for this mouse! Just show me the door and I'll never come back.*

Jack wanted to leave but could not find the strength to get up, as if his limbs were no longer taking mental orders from his brain. He rubbed his hands over his thighs to confirm his sensory perception was still intact. His numbness began to subside as he succumbed to a strange, eccentric curiosity to hear what Jonathan had to say. "Mr. Edwards, I suppose you'll tell me soon enough why you fooled me into meeting you here, today."

"Fooled you, Jack?" Jonathan asked in a tone of adolescent innocence. "I didn't fool you. I told you my name and asked you to join me for lunch. It was you that suggested the restaurant. I merely let you think what you wished."

"But you lied to me! You told me—"

Just as Jack started his accusation, Myra came back with their tea. "Here you go," she said, setting their glasses down.

"Thank you," they both responded.

"Your food order is in, and it'll be out in just a few minutes," she added. "Is there anything else I can get for you?"

"Not right now," Jonathan said. He waited for her to leave the table and then turning to Jack, "You were saying, Jack."

"I was saying that you lied to me," Jack said, pointing his finger, yet not raising his voice. "You told me you needed some new equipment. Why would the sales manager of Gantly need to buy equipment from Landover when Gantly can provide basically the same thing?"

"Jack, please. I didn't lie to you," Jonathan said in a smooth, calming, almost father-to-son like voice.

"Mr. Edwards," Jack started, with a confused expression, as he fumbled with his lap napkin, "you're going to have to spell this out for me. I don't understand what it is you're after."

"Let me get to the point." Jonathan's voice changed to a more business tone, as he unfolded his napkin and laid it in his lap. "I do need equipment, but it's not machinery, it's people." Jonathan sipped from his tea. "Jack, I need you."

Jack's jaw dropped. "You need me, Mr. Edwards? For what?"

"I need a tough salesman who isn't afraid of anything or anyone, and I've seen that in you."

"What do you mean; you've seen it in me? You don't even know me."

"I know almost everyone in this business," Jonathan shared with him, as Jack managed to gather his wits about him. "Most of the people you've met in this area during your little more than two years at Landover, I've either watched them grow up or watched them grow old and die. I know all the customers and, in many cases, their parents or their children, or both. I know the jobs you win, and I know the jobs we win, which, by the way, have been dwindling, thanks to you. So, congratulations on your victories, you've earned them," Jonathan conceded.

"Thank you, Mr. Edwards," Jack accepted.

Jonathan gestured a business salute to Jack, who was now mesmerized listening to Jonathan's oration. "You know, Jack, I've been around a long time. The business has changed a lot, the equipment that is, but not the salesman. As salesmen, we love taking a customer by the hand, leading him down a lily-lined path to places he never wanted to go, and getting him to buy things he doesn't absolutely need, all the while convincing him we're doing this in his best interest. Each of these mystical journeys reaches a euphoric climax with an authorized signature on the dotted line, covered, of course, by either cash or a suitable line of credit." He grinned. "We still work long hours, chase endless leads, generate redundant paperwork for customers who can't file—which is most of them—talk to people we don't like, and associate with those we don't share anything in common with except their money. We have a drive, Jack, that gets us up every morning for more of the same; a drive that inspires us to win. We love winning! It's a part of who we are. We love winning so much that we often forget there are rules involved." Jack was taken aback by the comment. "But sometimes the rules become our obstacles," Jonathan admitted. "Salesmen must be flexible, agile, ready to make a deal at any moment, and able to turn those obstacles into opportunities. The slightest hesitation often means the difference between winning and losing a job, and most salesmen fail to recognize this." Jonathan's speech was becoming more passionate. "Most people, Jack, can't appreciate the pressure a salesman is under to produce, so they ignorantly limit his innovativeness and productivity by shackling him with chains of policies, regulations, and procedures, all weighted down in bureaucracy and paperwork. We oftentimes have to shed those chains, those heavy weights, to realize our full potential, and once we've been freed from this corporate-regulated bondage, we have the freedom to do what we do best—make the sale. Do we cross the line at times? Yes! Yes, we cross the line! But it's all about the result of getting that contract endorsed with a legally authorized signature. Nothing else matters. Many say, 'Nothing happens until something is sold,' but I say nothing happens until I sell something!" Jonathan lightly rapped the table with his fist just as he said, 'I', the last time, awakening and reminding him of his surroundings. Jack had not moved a muscle in the last few minutes, as Jonathan's soliloquy had captured his undivided attention. Jonathan leaned back in his seat and removed his handkerchief from his suit coat to dab his dry brow. "Sorry, Jack. I guess I got carried away."

"That's alright, Mr. Edwards," Jack said, trying to make light of Jonathan's apparent embarrassment. "We all get carried away at times. That's what makes us salesmen."

"Indeed. That's what makes us salesmen," Jonathan agreed, nodding his head. He leaned forward and said, "Jack, I told you I need a salesman like you, and I meant it. I need someone who can make a deal. I need someone who can close a deal. I need someone who can steal a deal."

"But, Mr. Edwards," Jack offered, "I'm not sure if I'm the right guy for you."

Jonathan grinned. "Jack, do you remember the Stanford account?"

"Sure, I remember. It was a large portion of my last quarter sales."

"That job was worth over two-hundred-thousand dollars. My salesman had a firm verbal commitment from the purchasing agent on Friday afternoon, and on the following Monday morning we learned Landover had been awarded the job." Jonathan leaned a little more forward and changed to a more serious tone of voice. "Now, you and I both know what happened."

"You don't know anything about that job," his voice getting a little louder as he raised his defenses.

Jonathan remained calm, as he relaxed a bit. "It seems the purchasing-agent's wife is a lover of fine jewelry." Jack's facial expression changed from disdain to despair. "It's amazing what a diamond bracelet and set of half-carat diamond earrings will get you these days, isn't it, Jack?"

Jack sat in a silent stare, and then began fidgeting with his napkin. "Okay, Mr. Edwards," Jack admitted, "so I've done a few things outside the box. But you said yourself that we have to do what we can to make the sale." *After all, Jonathan's a professional, and if he's okay with it....*

"Jack," Jonathan pleaded, gesturing with his hands, "I'm on your side with this. I know what it takes to make a deal sometimes, and I'm okay with that. You see, you and I are innovators; we have both taught ourselves how to achieve success despite the overwhelming, day-to-day struggles we are subjected to by corporate policymakers. The difference is, I'm captain of my ship, and you're a first mate waiting to be discovered—someone who needs a change." Jack felt uneasy, as Jonathan leaned into the table. "By whom would you rather be discovered: me, one who offers you the chance of a lifetime, or your supervisor, who may not fully appreciate your, albeit rudimentary, self-guided sales approach?" Jack's blank stare answered the question. "I'll repeat what I said earlier," Jonathan continued, as he leaned back into his seat, "I want you to come to work for me. Consider this your long-awaited opportunity. So, what do you say? Do you want to get what you deserve?"

"Mr. Edwards, I certainly wasn't expecting this!" *Don't rush it, don't rush it. There are probably others who appreciate your skills and talent. If you wait you can have your choice.* "I feel I should jump at the chance, but can I have some time to think about it?" Jack's mind was in overload as he considered the possibilities.

"Of course, Jack! Take a few days, a week, two weeks. But I'll need to know something before too long."

"Sure, Mr. Edwards, I'll give it some thought and get back with you as soon as possible."

Just as Jack finished talking, their food arrived. "Here we are, gentlemen," Myra said, as she arranged her serving tray. "The grilled salmon for you," as she set Jonathan's plate in front of him, "and the T-bone and salad for you," setting Jack's plate down.

"Anything else," she asked, as she refilled their glasses.

"I think we're all just fine, now," Jack said with a grin, looking at Jonathan.

"Enjoy," Myra said, as she walked away.

"Mmm." Jonathan sounded at the dish before him, rubbing his hands together. "Grilled salmon never smelled so good. Your steak looks good, too, Jack."

"It certainly does," Jack replied. "Tell me something, Mr. Edwards," Jack asked, just as Jonathan was about to take a bite of his salmon. "How did you know about the bracelet and earrings?"

Jonathan lowered his fork and smiled. "His wife didn't like the watch I bought her." They both chuckled. "I hope you did well on that job. I bet that jewelry set you back a bit."

"Not really," Jack said, chewing his steak. "It was all cubic zirconia."

"What a pair we are," Jonathan said, as they both broke out in laughter.

Chapter 5

Lunch was Tom's favorite part of the workday, but today's one-hour escape was from more than his crowded calendar and endless phone calls. He and Chris tried to have lunch together on Fridays as often as their schedules allowed, and it was good to have a friend like Chris for days like this.

Today they tried a new restaurant, featuring a small, Tex-Mex buffet, which they took full advantage of before heading back to the office. The lunch conversation was lighter than normal, considering when they were both eating there was little talking at all.

Once in the car, Chris broke the awkward silence as Tom drove out of the restaurant parking lot. "I didn't want to say anything to spoil your lunch, but, man, Jonathan was pretty upset at you earlier. What did you do to make him so angry?"

"What makes you think he was angry?"

"Those loud reverberations told me someone wasn't happy."

"I guess those acoustically-thin walls between our offices don't hide much, do they?"

"Not at those decibel levels. I bet I could've registered the desk pounding on a Richter scale."

"I guess it was just my lucky day," he answered, as he shared his attention between Chris and the roadway ahead of them. "Jonathan places a lot of unrealistic expectations on all of us, hoping, I guess, he'll be able to clone copies of himself, not realizing that we're all different. He has a particular way of doing business, and I choose to do my business a different way, my way. I know he has a lot of experience, and we can all learn a lot from him, but there are a few things I wish he would keep to himself. In fact, I'm sure there are some things I don't even want to know how he does them."

"What do you mean?"

"For instance, right now we're working hard to capture that large Hartford account that should be released within the next two months, and I'm getting the impression that Jonathan wants me to …I mean …he …never mind." Tom looked straight ahead over the steering wheel.

"Sounds pretty serious. He's not wanting you to go tap dance outside the guy's office until he gives you a purchase order, is he?"

"I wish," Tom laughed. "That would make more sense, and it wouldn't be as embarrassing if I made the news."

"News? It's nothing illegal, is it?"

"Tap dancing? Fred Astaire never got arrested for it."

"No! What Jonathan wants you to do."

"Illegal?"

"Yeah, you know: against the law, jail, prison, time behind bars."

"No! It's not illegal!" *Is it?* "Illegal? No! Not even Jonathan would stoop that low, I don't think. Do you think he would?"

"You've known him longer than I have, but I get the feeling he could be pretty convincing to customers, if you know what I mean."

"Maybe we should change the subject before it digresses into one of Richard's conspiracy theories."

"Amen, to that," Chris agreed, "he can really go off the rails sometimes. Remember the time when Richard thought the shoe manufacturers were making his shoes smaller just so he would spend more money on a larger size?"

"Are you kidding? I was there when he tried to return them. The look on his face was priceless when the salesman removed the packing paper from the toe ends and said, 'Try them now, sir.' Richard put them on, thanked him for the adjustment, and we left."

"A different kind of guy for sure, and a good salesman," Chris admitted. "Quirks and all, he has a lot going for him."

"One big thing he has going for him is he never seems to have any such colorful confrontations with Jonathan."

"Look, I'm sure whatever is going on between you and Jonathan you'll do what's right, and God will get you through it. I know I can't offer you much advice on the business end, as you're more experienced than I am, but, if you need someone to talk to, about anything, you know you can count on me."

"Thanks, Chris, you're a great friend."

"I know; that's what I do." They both laughed. "By the way," Chris remembered, "Dana called me earlier today and wanted to know if you guys would like to come over tomorrow night for dinner."

"Sounds great. I'll call Linda when we get back to the office and make sure it's okay. I could sure use some unwinding."

"I know what you mean. This has been one tough week. I lost my good pen, one of my shoestrings broke yesterday, I can't find my pencil sharpener ..." Chris stopped short, as Tom cut his eyes over at him. "What?" Chris asked.

"You lost your pencil sharpener? I don't see how you've made it all week," he jested. *Leave it to Chris to keep me from taking life too seriously. Thank you, Lord, for his friendship.*

Before they knew it, they were back at the office. Tom parked his car, turned off the ignition, and removed his keys. He and Chris sat there for a moment, as each had their reasons for not wanting to get out right away. Tom sat with a blank forward stare, trying to imagine how much of the hollering his other coworkers had heard, while Chris looked at his watch, wanting to be sure he got his full hour in for lunch. "I guess we better get back at it," Chris said. "I've got a lot of paperwork to get caught up with before the weekend."

They exited the vehicle and walked inside, Tom lingering behind. Though this was the same facility they had left for lunch, everything seemed different now. He knew others had probably heard some version of the loud verbal lashing and could almost feel their pitiful stares as he made his way down the hall. A little embarrassed, Tom felt like it was his first day on the job, working with a bunch of strangers.

He entered his office and closed the door behind him. He leaned his back against the door with both hands on the doorknob and closed his eyes. He released a heavy sigh and stood there for a moment, then walked over to his desk and sunk into his office chair, not sure what to do next. He leaned all the way back, closed his eyes, and imagined the panorama of his office layout before him, as he began to rotate his chair in slow circles: door, coatrack, wall, bookshelf, pictures, desk, phone, door, coatrack, wall, bookshelf.... The phone ring pierced the silence. Tom tried to eject himself from his chair, but his momentum caused the chair to flip backward, striking the object behind him. Then he remembered, "Oh yeah, filing cabinet." With cat-like reflexes and a little disoriented, he rolled onto the floor and crawled to his desk. He pulled himself up on his knees, cleared his throat, and picked up the receiver. "Sales, this is Tom. How may I help you?" He moved the receiver away from his mouth so his body could stabilize from this short cardio workout.

"Hey, it's me," Linda, replied. Tom closed his eyes and relaxed his muscles; thankful it wasn't a customer. "I wanted to call to see what you were up to."

"Nothing much, just picking up a few things," he responded in a mellow tone, as he stood, brushed off his clothes, and surveyed his office floor. "What are you up to?"

"I was wondering if there's anything special you'd like to have for dinner."

"Not really," Tom replied. He noticed a new dent in the filing cabinet as he righted his chair, inspected the headrest, and sat down. "Anything will be fine."

"Is everything okay?"

"Sure," he answered. "Why do you ask?"

"You sounded a little down."

"I was," he laughed, "but I picked myself up."

"I don't get it," she responded.

"I meant your phone call picked me up." *I guess you had to be here.*

"Are you sure everything's okay?"

"Yes, honey," he said, "everything's fine. I'll see you tonight. Okay?" Just as he began to lower the receiver, he remembered Chris's dinner invitation. "Oh, wait! I almost forgot. Chris and Dana have invited us over for dinner tomorrow night. You want to go?"

"Sure. What time?"

"I didn't think to ask."

"Are their kids going to be there, or at Dana's mother's house?"

"I didn't ask that, either. You'd better call Dana and get all the details. I'm sure my mom will watch the kids if we need someone. Besides, if kids aren't allowed, it will be nice to have a free evening." Tom hung up the phone and fell back into his chair, cupping his hands over his face. This day had already been one of the longest he could remember in recent months, and he still had to make it through the afternoon. Trying to be positive, he was thankful Jonathan had chosen to browbeat him on a Friday, hoping the weekend would erase his embarrassment and help his coworkers forget the incident entirely. He spun his chair around to audit his office items, stopping at the filing cabinet. "Right after coatrack, but before wall. Got it."

"Where'd you guys go for lunch?" Richard asked Chris in the hallway.

"Oh, we tried the new Tex-Mex buffet place just down the road a few miles."

Richard followed him into his office. Chris took his seat behind his desk and Richard took a seat across from him. "Yeah, that's what this area needs is another Tex-Mex place," he said, rolling his eyes. "It's not like we don't have one on every corner. We need some variety in this area."

"It was better than a lot of other places we typically go to around here."

"That'll probably change after they've been open for a while and they think the word has spread to everyone in the area about their good food. That's the same thing that happened with the barbecue place that opened about a year ago. It's called the old bait-and-switch routine. They bait you with the good stuff then, later, they switch to the bad stuff."

"Why would any restaurant want to serve bad food?"

"Lots of reasons: cut costs, increase profits, lower expectations. They've got it all figured out."

Chris wanted to laugh, but Richard seemed so serious. "But wouldn't poor quality also run off some of their customers?"

"Not necessarily. They can move the good food in and out of service as the need arises. When they start seeing the numbers drop, they serve better food. I'm telling you, it's an old game in the restaurant business. I witnessed this when I worked as a waiter one summer while in college, and the experience taught me everything I need to know to fully understand the food-service industry."

"Wow! A whole summer, huh? Do you think it might have something to do with a person eating at the same place so often that they just get used to the taste of the food?"

"No way. I can eat at any restaurant in this area and tell when they're changing the quality of the food on their menus, and it almost always follows the trend for the size of the crowd. It's really not that hard to detect."

"Given your experience," Chris said smiling, "you might consider a career as a food-critic columnist, or a news reporter for the food-service industry. For us, we really enjoyed the food, and we'll probably go back soon. But we'll keep our taste buds open to all these alleged restaurant shenanigans and let you know if any of them play out."

"Give it a few months, and then don't say I didn't warn you when you discover the food doesn't taste the same."

They both sat for a few moments, as Richard took a casual glance at his fingernails, and Chris tried to think of a way to change the subject. "So, how's your Martindale proposal going?"

"I think they're using me."

"What do you mean?"

"They asked me to turn in a bid package, so I did, and I haven't heard from them since."

"Isn't that job a sealed-bid proposal, where all the bids are to be submitted by a certain date and then all are opened at a later, appointed time before all the participants?" Chris asked, to be sure.

"Sure, but those are always shady."

"On a sealed-bid proposal, they don't open the bids until a specific date and time, right?"

"That's the way it's supposed to work. But you never know what these guys do with the bids they receive before the opening date. There always seems to be a brother-in-law involved somewhere in these type deals, and I never seem to even be in the family tree."

"Look at the bright side. You're still in the hunt at least until the bid date."

"There's nothing magical about the bid date," Richard quipped. "If they've already picked who they want to have the job I won't win even if I give our stuff away. The process is just a formality to make it all seem more legit than what it is. I feel like I wasted my time putting the bid packet together. If they wanted me to have that job, I'd know by now."

Chris took a moment to collect his own sanity. "How would you know before the bid date whether you got the job or not?"

"Believe me. I know how these things work. I've been selling for a few years now, and I've discovered it's not that difficult of a vocation to follow."

"I'm sure your experience will also tell you things often turn out different than you expect. Why not hold out hope until the bid date? It certainly can't hurt anything."

"Yeah, and I'll put a tooth under my pillow and carry a rabbit's foot, too! I'm savvy enough to know this job is toast, so why worry about it. Besides, if I'm wrong, I'm wrong, which I doubt."

"Even if you don't get the Martindale job, you just turned in that order for your new customer, Southerland Works. That's a pretty decent order."

"Yeah, if the credit department lets it go through." Chris closed his eyes momentarily. "You have to wonder, sometimes," Richard continued, "just what they're up to. I got an e-mail message from them this morning to give them a call about that sale. I'm guessing I've got to dig up another page of Southerland's financial information, or their credit didn't get approved. Either way, it's just another shining example of the hassles you have to go through around here to make a sale."

"Remember, they have an obligation to protect the company finances. I'm sure they don't purposefully intend to block your sale."

"They don't have to block it, just keep me running all over town long enough gathering additional documentation until the customer decides to buy from someone else."

"You must be a hoot at family reunions."

"Don't get me started on that. The stories about my family are legendary where I come from. I have an uncle that—"

"As much as I've enjoyed the conversation, Richard," Chris interrupted, "I really need to get back to work."

"What's the hurry?" Richard asked. "It's not like you're going to get a whole lot more done today, anyhow. It's Friday, for crying out loud. You think all the managers are hard at work at anything besides trying to put together a foursome on the local golf course for tomorrow?"

"Despite the fact that it is Friday, we still have an obligation to put in a full day's work. Besides, as a Christian, I'm not going to let my ethics or character be dictated by which day of the week it is."

"I didn't say I wasn't going to work," Richard responded. "I've got things to do, too, you know. In fact," he continued as he stood up and straightened his tie, "I've got a couple of bids I need to get completed before the weekend, so I've got to go."

"I'll see you around, Richard." Chris sighed with relief as Richard left his office. "Note to self;" he said. "Don't open the can if you can't keep the worms in."

Chapter 6

"What time is it?" Paula asked.

"It's about 9:30," Jack replied, reading the morning newspaper. "Warren should be here any minute. I'm glad he didn't have to work this Saturday so he could help me paint the nursery."

"That is, if you guys actually get busy, instead of just sitting around all day watching television."

"Oh, come on, honey. Warren's my best friend and we like hanging out together, but I know how important the nursery is to you. I've got all the prep work done just like he instructed me and all the materials on hand to take care of everything. It's all under control, and we'll do a great job, I promise."

"I'm about to leave to go get Jenny and then we're headed out to go shopping. I'm just finishing up some snacks for you guys to keep you from rummaging all through the refrigerator. They're on the kitchen counter on a covered dish." Paula finished cleaning up in the kitchen and walked into the living room. She picked up her purse and car keys just as they heard a knock on the door with a familiar rhythm. "Sounds like he's here." Jack stood up as they both made their way to the front door, and Jack opened it.

"Hey, Warren, come on in."

Warren entered the room dressed to go to work in his light, long-sleeved, collarless pullover, overalls, and a ball cap with his company logo. His high-school football days were long gone but his naturally large frame was still quite intimidating to many, as it filled most of the doorway. His close friends knew his size only hid the fact he was just a big teddy bear. "Hey guys," Warren replied. "How's it goin'?"

"Now remember," Paula said, looking at Warren and pointing her finger, "no goofing off today. The room needs to be finished."

"Oh, yes ma'am," Warren replied, with a touch of sarcasm.

"Warren!"

"I'm sorry, Paula," Warren answered, smiling. "We'll be finished today, I promise. Besides, there's no football on TV to distract us."

"I'm going shopping with Jenny while you two get busy painting the nursery." She kissed Jack before stepping out the door. Looking back, she asked, "What time do you think you guys will be done?"

"I'd say about two O'clock," Jack replied.

"Don't listen to him," Warren cautioned. "He's not a professional like me. We'll probably be finished around 1:55." Then, noticing Paula was not smiling, he added, "We'll be finished by two O'clock."

"Good. I'll be back around three. Bye, hon," she said to Jack.

"Bye, hon."

"Bye, mom," Warren said. Paula smiled as she left, while Jack closed the door.

"Okay, Warren, where do you want to start?"

"You have all the materials, right?" he asked, as they walked to the nursery.

"I think I've got everything here we'll need. I even stayed up late last night and covered the floor with plastic and taped off the window."

Warren gave it all a close examination. "It looks like you've done all the hard work," he said, as he admired Jack's preparation. "All we need to do is throw the paint on. We should be done in a couple of hours, long before they leave the first shoe store."

"I was thinking that if we get the painting out of the way first thing, we can let the house air out until Paula gets home so the smell won't be so bad. Paula doesn't need to be around wet paint any more than she has to in her condition."

"Speaking of condition, how's your job going? You said last night on the phone that you had another opportunity or something like that."

"I haven't made up my mind yet," Jack said, as he began lining up some paint cans in the back of the room, while Warren gathered paint trays and brushes. "The company I'm working for has been good to me, but I feel I have more to offer. Now, out of the blue, I get an invitation to work for a competitor that will allow me to use all my …talents. From all indications, it seems like it'll be a great deal for me and Paula, possibly offering as much as a thirty-percent salary increase, including commissions that is."

"What's holding you back? It sounds like your ship has finally come in."

"Perhaps. I'm still thinking about it. The man said he needed an answer within about two weeks, so I'm trying to decide if it's time to make a change. If not, I'll stay where I am." Then, looking over at Warren, "You must be doing pretty good." Jack gave a lazy punch to Warren's arm. "I noticed you have another new truck."

"Yeah, I just got it last Thursday."

"But didn't you already have a new truck?"

"Yeah, but I got bored with it and traded it in. You should get you one."

"I'm not in a position to be financially able to afford a new truck right now."

"Oh, come on. If I can afford one, you can, too."

"What makes you think I can afford a new truck?"

"You make just as much money as I do. I don't understand what the problem is."

"Let's see," Jack began, "I'm married, and you are ..." He waited for Warren's response.

"Single!"

"Yes, you're single."

"But I have a fiancée," he added. "Isn't that the same thing?"

"Let's compare the two and see," Jack continued. "Who pays for her apartment rent?"

"She does. Why should I? I don't live there."

"Who pays her car payment?"

"She does. It's not my car."

"Okay. Who buys her clothes?"

"She does, and she loves to wear nice things. I wouldn't spend that kind of money for clothes. That alone could break a fella."

"Who buys her groceries?"

"She does, and that health food she eats is also expensive."

"Yeah, Warren," Jack said, tilting his head and exhibiting a face of deep thought as he rubbed his chin, "I'd say, financially speaking, a wife is pretty comparable to a fiancée."

"Gotcha, Jack!" Warren offered an enthusiastic high-five, which was met with a lazy swing in the air from Jack, who stared in bewilderment.

Jack managed a perplexed look while Warren continued to celebrate. *Did he not hear a word I said?*

"Maybe I need to be talking to Paula about this truck thing," Warren said. "I think she understands money better than you do. And I'm not sure what all those questions had to do with you buying a truck. From what I see, you and I are on about the same financial plain," Warren declared, as his cell phone rang. He pulled it from his pocket to check the caller ID. "It's my mother. Excuse me for just a minute." Warren turned away as he answered his phone. "Hi, Mom." He listened as she responded. "I should be home at about six O'clock," he answered. "I'm just helping Jack get his nursery painted then I'm going to go get a new multimedia system installed in my truck." He waited for his mother to finish talking. "That'll be fine, Mom, whatever you and Dad want. Alright. I'll see you later this afternoon." He hung up the phone and turned to face Jack.

"She just wanted to know what to fix for supper tonight. I hope she doesn't get mad when she goes to my room to get my dirty clothes. She made me finish my breakfast this morning and it put me a little behind, so, I didn't get a chance to straighten up my room before I left."

Jack was almost numb from listening to Warren's conversation. *Same financial plain? If we're on the same plain, then he's on the end with the enchanted forest and I'm foraging the parched land for nuts and wild berries!* "Come on, Warren," Jack said. "Let's get started or we'll never finish."

"Absolutely." Warren was pumped up. "Let's do this thing," he said, as he slapped his hands together.

"By the way, Paula made some snacks for us to eat after we're done."

"Then let's do this thing quickly."

Tom spent Saturday morning working in the yard, still thinking of Jonathan's verbal thrashing. He seemed to push the lawnmower a little faster than normal, despite the extra growth from the recent rains earlier in the week. Not exactly a small, residential lot, about a quarter of an acre, but the large number of trees and his desire for hard work made a push mower the obvious choice. It had been a while since the hedges had been trimmed, but he was finished with them in a short time. A few of the trees required a modest amount of trimming, and the limbs made quite a stack at the street curb. The gutters got a fresh flush to clear last year's leaves and runoff from the roofing shingles.

Finally, six hours later, it was all done. He pulled off his leather work gloves and stood in his driveway in a satisfying sweat and took just a moment to look around and admire his work. He had cut, pruned, bundled, and cleaned in hopes that something better would come of it. *Why can't life be just as easy, to cut and trim the bad and keep the good?* Then he remembered. *That's what God does for His children; He prunes our lives that we might grow and mature in His will. Thank you, Lord.*

"Tom!" Linda called from the front door. "Don't forget we have a few errands to run before we go over to Chris and Dana's."

"I'll be there in just a little bit."

"My goodness, Tom," Linda said smiling, as she walked out the front door and admired the landscape and the large wood pile at the curb, "you've done quite a bit of work this morning, and it all looks beautiful."

"Yeah. I haven't done this much yard work in a long time."

"I'll say. There's enough wood on the curb to start a small bond fire. What got into you?"

"You know I work harder when I'm thinking," he kidded.

"You must have a lot to think about."

"I'm really just trying to work through something at work."

"Nothing bad, is it?"

"Oh, no!" *Why did I say anything? Now she'll worry!* "It's just something that requires a lot of thought, that's all."

"Have you prayed about it?"

"Many times. I can't understand why God doesn't answer."

"Maybe you're waiting for your answer and not willing to accept His."

Linda's comment struck a chord. "You always seem to have the right thing to say." He leaned over and kissed her. "I guess I better get cleaned up."

"You're telling me. You sweat like a racehorse, but you smell like an old hound dog. I'll go in and fix you something cold to drink." Linda walked back into the house while Tom watched her all the way.

Physically exhausted, he put away his lawn implements and cleaned his chain saw. Lastly, he pushed the mower into the garage and stood still for a moment before releasing the handle, his mind starting to drift as he closed his eyes. "Lord," he prayed, "I need your wisdom on what to do. Please help me to submit my life to You, that You might be able to perform Your good work in me, whatever that might be." Tom finished his prayer of surrender and opened his eyes. His concerns seemed to subside, as he felt a deep, inner peace, and then he realized he had finally given God what He wanted—a willing heart. Now he felt he had a better idea of what God was leading him to do.

Later that evening, Tom and Linda were ready to relax and have a good time at the Damans with all the kids visiting their respective grandparents, so it was just Chris, Tom, and their wives at dinner. Both families enjoyed their children, but it was nice to have an evening occasionally with other adults to discuss adult matters. Most of the time, however, the adult matters ended up being a discussion about all the kids.

Shortly after Tom and Linda arrived, dinner was served. Dana had prepared her special spaghetti and meatballs with a flavorful sauce from an old family recipe. For dessert, there was key lime pie, and carrot cake, one of Tom's favorites. Conversation was not short during the meal, as they each enjoyed one another's company, though Tom and Chris were careful to minimize the shoptalk.

Following dinner, Chris invited Tom out back to sit by the pool, while Linda and Dana sat at the dining table swapping their own child-rearing horror stories. Tom also thought it would be another opportunity for Linda to witness to Dana about her soul. Though she and the kids attended church with Chris, she was not a Christian but was warming up to Linda's conversations.

"That was an excellent dinner, Chris," Tom said, as they carried their tea out by the pool and closed the patio door behind them.

"Thanks, Tom. I wish I could take the credit, but that's all Dana's doing. Have a seat," he said, pointing at the new patio chairs and tables. "We just got these last week, and we love them. They recline, too."

"They sure look nice," Tom commented as they each selected a chair and sat down. Tom set his glass on the small table between them and leaned back to get the full impact of its comfort, while running his hands along the arm rests to check for sturdiness. "And these weatherproof cushions feel great, too." He glanced over at the cushions in the other chairs around the pool, and then looked closer at the ones he was sitting on. Then looking over at Chris, "Please tell me this was the only pattern available for these cushions," he ribbed, "as I'm sure you would have preferred something a little less princess-like."

"I know, I know." Chris acknowledged. "But Dana and the kids love them, so this is what we went with." Chris set his glass on the table and reclined his chair to help him stretch out. "Ahhh! This is nice. Just sitting around and relaxing, forgetting all your worldly cares, if only for a little while."

Tom sat fidgeting with his chair cushions and looking around the pool area, trying to find a way to bring up what was on his mind. "Chris?"

"Yeah, buddy," Chris replied, resting his eyes, and stretching his neck muscles.

"Remember yesterday, after lunch, you said I could talk to you about anything?"

"Sure, Tom. What is it?" he asked without opening his eyes, still pivoting his head side to side.

"It's about Jonathan."

"Oh, no! Not Jonathan! Anything but Jonathan!" Chris lamented, as he laid his head back in his chair and covered his face with both hands.

"Come on, man, be serious." Tom sat up.

"Oh, sorry, Tom," Chris apologized. He looked at Tom with a semi-straight face.

"First of all, I've got to have your word that you'll keep this to yourself. I don't want it to get out to anyone else at work, and certainly not to Linda until I'm ready to tell her."

"Sure, sure, Tom."

Tom took a moment to deliver his statement. "I think I've made up my mind to leave Gantly," he said in one fluid exhale.

Chris was quiet while he cataloged what Tom had said. Once it sunk in, "What? Are you crazy?" he blurted out, as he sat up in total surprise. They both turned toward the patio door and stared for a moment to be sure their wives did not hear his response. Seeing no reaction, "Are you crazy?" he repeated at a much lower volume. Tom widened his eyes, a little shocked at Chris's initial response. "You're the biggest sales producer we have, which probably comes with a pretty big paycheck to match. You're willing to give all that up?"

"Money's not everything, Chris," Tom admitted, "you know that. There's something to be said for peace of mind, and you can't buy that." Tom stood up and made his way over by the pool, admiring the indirect lighting along the walking path. His eyes followed the colorful stone tiles outlining the irregularly shaped perimeter before glancing down to find the pool skimmer—not hard with all the underwater lighting—now located at the bottom of the deep end. The cool, night air told him it was a little early for swim season, but it was evident Chris would have everything ready to go when the time came. He placed his hands in the pockets of his light jacket, thankful he had remembered to bring it. "Believe me, I've tried. I used to reward myself with gadgets and gizmos, thinking I had earned them for putting up with Jonathan, hoping they would relieve the stress from the day-to-day interactions with him, but, to no avail. I discovered that none of them really satisfied. I was just using them as a diversion from the real issue; I needed to grow up spiritually. Finally, I've learned there's no greater piece of mind than knowing you're in the will of God."

After a short silence, Chris asked, "I guess you've thought this through and prayed about it?"

Tom turned to face Chris. "Yes. And I believe God has given me peace to make a change." Tom began pacing back and forth, dipping his head, and staring off as he talked. "I've done my best over the years to work under Jonathan's management style, but it's starting to get to me. I've prayed for patience to endure his remarks and for wisdom to know how to respond, but it's just not happening. The atmosphere wasn't too bad when Malcolm was around, just a rude comment here and there, a small outburst once in a while. But after Malcolm left, Jonathan was bitter, and he seemed to take it out on me and Donavan." Tom reflected for a moment as he stared out at the pool. "Did I ever tell you he waited a year after Malcolm left before hiring Richard? Just out of the blue one day, Malcolm gets an offer from a guy in Arkansas—an old college roommate—that would more than double his salary, and he took it. I thought it was a great opportunity for him, but Jonathan came unglued! Somehow, he was able to convince Charles that Malcolm's position was unnecessary anyway, that his leaving was a good thing, and he tried to cover the extra sales territory himself, as best he could, to help validate his illusion. It worked for a while, but then the construction market eventually picked up, and he couldn't keep covering for the loss in sales and the increased frequency of customer complaints. His story was that he actually grew the business to the point to where we needed to hire another salesman, which Charles bought into, and that's when he hired Richard." Tom kicked around a few small rocks at his feet. "Huh," he snickered. "Now that I think about it, I've never known Jonathan to have a run-in with Richard; at least, nothing outside his customary supervisor rhetoric."

"Not even at the beginning?"

"No. He continued to focus his ranting between me and Donavan, and then Donavan quit a few months later, leaving me to take the brunt of his verbal abuse. I thought it would be short-lived, and maybe die off once his bitterness subsided, but it hasn't yet."

"Did it get any worse after Donavan left?"

"Not really. But it didn't get any better either. Hiring you to replace Donavan reduced the frequency of his instructional lectures, and their intensity; though, yesterday was the worst I can remember."

"Why do you think he's still doing it?"

"I'm not sure." Tom replied. "I know he's facing a lot of pressure from Charles to increase our sales numbers. Maybe he believes his negative remarks are supposed to motivate me to do better, or maybe he's trying to keep me from being as good as he believes he is, or once was. He put a lot of time and effort into training Malcolm as his protégé, so he may be afraid of getting too close to anyone else, fearful they'll quit, too. Unfortunately, his management style is working the opposite effect …at least on me. I'm not sure what his motive is but I'm tired of trying to figure it out."

"If you quit, do you suppose Jonathan will just find someone else to take his vengeance out on?"

"I don't know," Tom said. "I hope not, for your sake. Right now, it seems he's content to vent on me; after all, I'm the only one left from the Malcolm era. Maybe my leaving will cause him to be more respectful to others. Sometimes it takes situations like this to get people like Jonathan to wake up to the fact that what they are doing is not working. Who knows? It may also open a door for someone else to witness to him; God knows I've tried."

"I'll hate to see you leave, Tom, but I can understand why you feel like you need to. Let me know when you decide to let the hammer down."

"I will. Once God gives me a clear direction, I'll discuss it with Linda, and then I'll let you know. That way, you'll get first shot at my office furniture."

"I have always had a hankering for your coatrack," Chris joked. "So, what's the next step?"

"I want to stay in sales, I know that, and I love selling equipment; it's what I know best. I'm sure I could learn to sell almost anything, but I've always had a passion for selling equipment."

"Then you'll have to go to a competitor," Chris admitted.

"I know." Tom hung his head.

"Hey, don't worry about it, Tom. There's plenty of business out there for all of us, right?" After a short silence, "I guess we should go see what the ladies are up to."

"Thanks for listening, Chris," Tom said, as Chris stood. "I'd ask that you pray for me, that God would give me the job He wants me to have. It will certainly be on my mind tomorrow at church."

"Let's pray about it right now." They bowed their heads as Chris prayed out loud, and Tom thanked God for his caring friend.

Chapter 7

Monday mornings were busy for the Landover salesmen, starting with a sales meeting in the boardroom to discuss open business and potential leads. They met early, around 8:00am, so everyone could be on their way by 9:00am, at the latest. The meeting also gave everyone an opportunity to talk about what was and was not working in their respective sales areas, which encouraged new ideas and techniques.

Snacks were a staple of every sales meeting, and today it was bagels. "What's this, Paul?" Ben said, pointing at the tray of bagels.

"Never mind the jokes, fellas," Paul said smiling. "Just be happy there's something to chew on besides the tabletop."

"Yeah, but are they any more flavorful?" Tony joked.

"Or softer?" Ben added.

"Ha, ha, very funny," Paul replied.

"Don't take this personal, Paul," Jack said, "but we'd rather have donuts."

"My wife makes me eat these things once in a while, and I figure if I've got to eat them then you guys can eat them, too. So, dig in."

Tony picked through the selection. "I don't see any with fruit."

"How about any fruit remnants, even the smell of fruit, or a bagel shaped like fruit?" Ben asked.

"Nope, just plain, plain, or plain," Tony responded.

"That's alright," Ben said, after a firsthand inspection, "at least there are a few condiments to help add flavor. Cream cheese and coffee can help only so much." After a few minutes, everyone had made their selection and taken their seat, as the meeting began.

"This morning we're going to do things a little different from our normal routine," Paul started. "Let's not discuss any business this morning but rather share something personal with the group about ourselves."

Jack stopped chewing his bagel to be sure he heard Paul, should he repeat himself. *Did he say personal, or Percival? I don't know anyone named Percival.* He listened hard, hoping someone else would help him make the determination.

"Oh, no," Ben sighed. "We're not going to strip down to our underclothes and start beating on a drum, are we?" Everyone started laughing, including Paul. Jack just smiled; his ears still perked.

"Maybe we'll hold hands and sing songs about inner peace," Tony added.

"We're not getting that intimate," Paul assured them, still smiling. "It's just that I think sometimes we get into such a routine of doing our jobs that all our actions become so robotic, almost to the point that people become transparent to us, even those we work with. For example, we don't call Cheryl for information, we call the receptionist. We don't talk to Steven about a service issue, we talk to the service manager. In each of these examples we replace the person with a position, and the interaction becomes dehumanized and mechanical."

It's Personal, Jack thought, as he commenced chewing his bagel, a little disappointed in his finding. *What's next, counselors and confessionals?* He thought of Roy, one of his coworkers when he sold home appliances, who, in a similar situation, broke down in their sales meeting as he confessed to ripping off a few retail customers. *That's what happens when you expose your emotions.* Jack took a sip of coffee to help swallow the hard lump in his throat.

Paul continued. "Maybe we've trained ourselves to think that if we look at people as positions or inanimate objects, rather than human beings, we can pretend they don't have feelings or personal needs, and certainly none as important as our own. We find ourselves cutting people off in traffic, ignoring the greeting from the grocery cashier, talking down to coworkers, mocking those with lesser skills or abilities—all because we've decided they have no personal life quests and are incapable of helping us achieve ours. Maybe the driver you cut off owns the grocery store where you shop or is the principal where your child attends school. How different would we treat the slow-driving, gray-haired old man in front of us if we knew he was our father, our grandfather, or church elder?"

"Or younger brother in your case," Ben interjected, as the group broke out in laughter.

"I guess I should've seen that one coming," Paul said. "I thought if we each shared something personal this morning, as a group, it would help remind us why we're here. I know we all must have jobs, and we come here for a paycheck, but we also need to remember that we all have a purpose, and we work together as a team to help each other achieve our respective, personal goals. My work helps those around me, so, when I succeed, others do also."

I can do this, Jack thought. *Just throw out some good, positive stuff before it gets out of control, and move on.* "I'll go first," Jack offered. "I've got lots of good stuff going on in my life."

"I appreciate the enthusiasm, Jack, but I'd like to start with Ben, then Tony, and then you." Jack surrendered the floor, though a little agitated at the rejection of his offer. He had participated in these team-building confessionals before and knew it was not good to be too far down the batting order when it came time to speak. "So, Ben, if you don't mind, go ahead and get us started."

Jack crossed his fingers, hoping for the best. *Come on, Ben, let it be one of your crazy fishing or hunting stories.*

"As you all know, my wife and I are the proud parents of a new baby boy. He's three months old and never sleeps, at least not when I'm home. We knew what to expect when he was born, since we already had a healthy two-year-old: mid-morning feedings, dirty diapers, lost sleep, and everything else that goes with it." Then his smile disappeared. "But nothing could have prepared us for the news that our son has a degenerative eye disease that may diminish his sight before he's a teenager."

Jack closed his eyes as he dipped his head—*and it begins.*

"Man, was that earth shattering!" Ben continued. Then with a slight upbeat, he added, "But the doctors say there is a good chance special treatments could prevent the disease from progressing, allowing him to retain most of his sight; how much, no one knows. So, we keep praying he'll not get any worse."

After a short silence, "That's good, Ben," Paul said. "That's what I'm talking about, sharing something personal—something that maybe no one else in this group knows about."

Jack rolled his eyes, afraid he was beginning to feel a slight magnetic force drawing him to the fringe of sharing in this intimate, verbal exchange. *Why can't we just go back to work? It was personal enough when I knew only his shoe size.*

Paul continued. "I think it gives us a better appreciation for where others are in their life with their respective circumstances. I'm not asking you to share anything you don't feel comfortable sharing. You can make it as personal as you like. I appreciate your openness and honesty, Ben. My wife and I will certainly be praying for your son." Then turning to Tony, "Tony, what would you like to share with us?"

"I don't know what to say, now, after that. Nothing I have seems as significant."

"Exactly." Jack said. He picked up his pen and pad and motioned as if he was about to stand. "Maybe we should just gather our things and go take some time to consider—"

"That's just it!" Paul said, as Jack's comment went unheard. "What you have to say is significant!" Jack sank back down into his chair and rolled his eyes, realizing he was going to have to take his turn. His bagel lost its flavor, despite the strawberry-flavored cream cheese he had showered it with. "We can't let ourselves be fooled to believe that what each of us does is not important unless we are doing something really great, or that the circumstances we live in are not important unless they are a lot worse or much better than everyone else around us! We are a team, and we will only succeed as a team if we recognize the significance of each individual member! The circumstances surrounding your life should be just as important to you as the circumstances in anybody else's life are to them."

"Wow!" Ben interjected. "I didn't expect to cause such a ruckus, but you're right, Paul. I mean, my wife and I don't let this get us down. We know it's serious, but life must go on. We can't wait for everything around us to be perfect before we allow ourselves to be happy—it'll never happen—and we certainly don't expect others' lives to cave in when we come around them. We still laugh with our kids, joke around with our friends, and enjoy watching a good movie together. This is the life we've been given, and we choose to be honest with ourselves about it." Everyone sat quiet for a moment.

"That was a much better verbalization of what I've been trying to say, Ben. When we can admit and accept our individual position in life and are honest with ourselves, then we can be honest with those around us and see the importance each of us contributes. So, you see, Tony, what you have to say is important, because it's important to you."

"I'm kind of excited about me and my wife buying our first house," Tony said.

"Great!" Paul commented.

"That's fantastic!" Jack cried out, "Tony is getting a house. I think a house is a wonderful thing to discuss, so let's talk about that."

Jack garnered a few bewildered looks, before Tony continued. "We're supposed to close next week, which is why I asked off for next Thursday. Each of our parents is giving us one room of furniture. In fact, my wife is out shopping with her mom today."

"That's where it all starts," Ben interjected. "First, it's the free stuff from the in-laws, then it's no-holds-barred right from your own wallet. You'd better be careful."

"She'll do okay," Tony replied. "She's thriftier with money than I am."

"That's just great, Tony," Paul applauded. "Let us know when you start moving in so we can help. Right, guys?" he said to Ben and Jack.

"Oh, sure," they joked. "Wouldn't miss it."

"I think I'm busy that day," Ben jested.

"Jack, you're next. What have you got for us?"

By now, Jack felt like he was in the middle of an old-fashioned, all-too-familiar, tent revival meeting looking for a way out, just like he did as a child. *Why couldn't I go first?* "Uh, things have really taken off these last two years. I am fortunate to have been part of many good things, not only at Landover, but also in my personal life. My wife and I are expecting our first child in about four months, and we are all excited about that."

"I can recommend a good brand of earplugs," Ben said. "Trust me; morning comes much earlier with only three hours of sleep." They all laughed.

"I think what Ben is trying to say, in his own way, is life will never be the same," Paul added. "Anything else?"

"And I have the good fortune of working with you guys." *What was that? That was about the lamest thing I've ever said, including my acceptance speech after winning my third-grade turtle-race competition.* Jack tried to smile, hoping his feeling of ignorance was not being displayed on his face.

"Now that wasn't so bad, was it?" Paul asked the group. "I think we all learned something new—"

"No, no, no, no, Paul," they all interrupted.

"You didn't take your turn," Ben informed him.

"Oh! Sorry about that. I was so excited about how this was going I guess I overlooked myself. Let's see. As you all know, my wife and I have three children, all grown. Two are married and the third is in college and engaged, so, we're about to be empty nesters. I think that's going to be harder on my wife than it will be on me," he said, smiling. "We've lived in this area all our lives and don't plan on moving even after we retire."

"You mean you're not retired already?" Ben commented.

"Not yet, Ben," Paul acknowledged. "Anyway, I hope each of you enjoyed this morning. As I said before we started, it would be a little unusual, but I think it helps us to remember why we do what we do. Yes, it's for the money, but it's also for each other. It takes everyone working together for us to succeed, but only one of us not staying focused to bring us down." Jack dipped his head, as he wiped his hand across his mouth a few times. "That's all I have for you guys this morning. Help yourselves to the bagels. I'm sure others will be in here to pick from what's left. And have a good day."

Paul gathered his stuff together and noticed Ben going through the bagels. "Did you lose something, Ben?"

"Yeah," he replied. "I bit down on one of these bagels and I think I lost a tooth."

Ben and Tony smiled at each other. Paul just laughed as he opened the door and walked out of the room. Then, remembering he left his pen on the table, Paul immediately returned to the room, and there stood Jerry over the bagel tray. "Wow. Hey, Jerry, how's it going? Did I miss you in our meeting?"

"Oh no. I was down the hall when you guys broke up and I wanted to see what was left over."

Paul looked back at the door and back at Jerry. "But how did you …I mean.…"

"Great call on the bagels, Paul," Jerry said with a thumbs-up affirmation while he piled his bagel high with cream cheese.

"I gather you like bagels, Jerry?"

"There one of my favorite grain foods," he admitted, as he took his first bite.

"Help yourself to as many as you like." Paul found his pen and left the room.

"Mmm," Jerry moaned, as he tilted his head back, closed his eyes, and licked the cream cheese from his lips between chews on his bagel.

Tom started his Monday with a visit to a familiar customer, Torres Construction. They had a small, heavy-machinery operation in Haslet of about thirty-five employees that served most of north Texas and southern Oklahoma and had purchased a few small pieces of machinery from Tom over the years. It was a much closer drive for Tom to leave from his house, so he had also setup additional appointments in the area with other customers to make efficient use of his time. He had planned these visits a week ahead and was thankful they were today, since they would keep him out of the office and away from Jonathan, at least until noon.

Tom walked through the front door and into the lobby, where he was greeted by Janet, the receptionist. "Good morning, Tom. If you came by to see Albert, I'm afraid he just left to run some errands, and I have no idea when he may be back. Daniel's in, if you would like to see him?"

Before Tom could respond, he spied Daniel walking down the hall by the lobby area, reviewing some paperwork as he headed toward his office. When Daniel noticed a visitor in the lobby, he stopped and looked up to see a familiar face. "Tom!" he called out. Tom made his way over to greet Daniel. "You just missed Dad, and there's no telling how long he'll be gone. If you would like to wait around, you can come sit in my office. We'll find something to talk about."

"You got a deal," Tom responded. He turned back toward the lobby. "Thanks, Janet," he said, as Daniel escorted him back to his office.

An older teenager when Tom first met him, Daniel had become a very integral part of the Torres Construction operation. He grew up around the shop as a little boy and had always been fascinated by the large equipment, hoping someday work with his father. At sixteen, Albert hired Daniel to help in his repair shop. His natural mechanical ability and team leadership skills advanced him to his present position of shop leader.

Although he was a man in business, he was not yet a businessman. He knew the mechanical side of the job well, but the office procedures were still new to him. His visual organizational style was reflected in the stacks of paper lining the eight-foot, plastic table in his medium-sized office, dimly lit from the single fluorescent fixture in the center of the room. Each stack represented a job that was either still in a bidding process or was currently being worked in the field, differentiated only by the color of paperweight on top of its respective stack: blue for bids and white for working. Though, to Tom, Daniel's filing system seemed rather crude, it was an improvement to Albert's hide-and-seek process, which had caused a few billing errors in the past. Janet now handled all the invoicing, which increased their cash flow efficiency.

Daniel entered his primitive office and took a seat behind the desk—a wooden relic much older than himself—and Tom sat across from him. In all the years Tom had been calling on Torres Construction, nothing about the facilities had changed much. The furniture was the same, including the thirty-year-old, lightly cushioned, dining room chair he was sitting in, and it all looked old when Tom first visited six years ago. The carpet was the same and in need of replacement, evidenced by the trails worn all the way down the center of the hall and at the entrance of each office. The office walls appeared to have been painted countless times, and the lack of effort on the part of the painter to distinguish between trim and wall color was obvious. But Torres Construction did their best to keep everything clean and pleasant, especially the lobby.

Daniel leaned back in his comfortable office chair, as Tom tried to relax in his seat, though the fixed-frame chair resisted his every attempt. He knew his effort was futile, not knowing why he tried to get comfortable in the first place; after all, it was the same chair he had sat in each time he came to visit Daniel. During several past visits he had often thought of retrieving one of the more comfortable visitor chairs from Albert's office but didn't want to embarrass Daniel for his apparent lack of consideration for his guests—something Tom hoped Daniel would learn in time. Until then, he decided he would implement a time limit on his visits with Daniel to coincide with whichever came first: either the conversation was over, or he had lost all feeling in his lower extremities.

"So, what's up today, Tom?"

"I was hoping I could catch Albert this morning to discuss the equipment you guys bought about four months ago from Landover."

"Yeah, that was his project. He handles all the buying and selling of our major equipment. I just take care of all the field work, maintaining the equipment, and talking with customers." Daniel thought for a moment, and then expressed a puzzled look. "I don't know a whole lot about what transpired with that purchase contract, but what I do know about it, I don't understand. For starters, I thought we had made a deal with Gantly, which was fine with me because I like you guys, and you've always been fair with us. Then, a few days later Dad's telling me we should be expecting some Landover equipment soon. I didn't know at the time that this was the same deal. When it all went down, I asked Dad why he had changed his mind, and he told me he just got a better deal from Landover. So, I let it go at that."

"It was just as much a surprise to me, too, which is why I've been trying to see Albert. I know he's always busy, but it seems as though he's trying to avoid me."

"You know Dad. He's not one to discuss too much with anyone, especially business details."

"I saw some of your new equipment sitting outside when I drove up. You must have the rest out on jobs already."

"We bought five tractors total, and three are out working in different areas. I got spec sheets for all of them here on my desk. I was going over their maintenance requirements to be sure I order plenty of consumables to take care of them, you know: filters, belts, oils, etc." Daniel sat up and reached for the brochures and handed them to Tom one at a time as he sequentially listed them off. "We bought two of these smaller machines, two of these machines, and one of these. That last one is a big one. It went out on its first job today."

Tom glanced over the brochures, comparing the machines to Gantly's similar offerings. "Daniel, I'm a little concerned. Our original contract proposal was for four pieces of equipment—two each of the two smaller sizes, similar to the models shown on these two brochures." He handed Daniel the two brochures he was comparing. "We couldn't sell you anything that was comparable to the much larger machine in this third brochure." He handed the last brochure back to Daniel, who put all three back on the corner of his desk.

"Do you guys not offer anything that large?"

"Certainly, we do, but that wasn't the problem. In fact, Gantly and Landover provide almost the identical variety in equipment sizes and functionality. The problem was the line of credit Torres Construction had at the time would not support a purchase as large as the one you've made. In fact, Albert made it clear to me that he didn't want to overextend himself on this purchase, so buying any large equipment, though he needed it, was out of the question. He knew for Torres Construction to buy just the four smaller machines was a calculated risk, requiring at least a modest increase in work. That purchase itself would have made it rough around here, but manageable. When you throw in that larger machine, which probably adds at least another thirty percent to the total purchase price, it changes everything. He told me he could secure a loan from the bank, but the payments would have been astronomical. I hope Albert was able to get a good interest rate."

"Wow! You make it all sound pretty bad."

"Sorry, Daniel, that wasn't my intention. Before we both get carried away, why don't you talk with your dad about this. I'm sure he has a plan of action, just as he did for the smaller proposal. In the meantime, let's hope business picks up."

"We've definitely seen an increase in business, and it has been small so far, but it's getting better. We've been able to put some of the new equipment to work, but that's mostly because we have some older machinery that's down for repairs. I wonder how Landover was able to work around the larger contract."

"Remember, Daniel, companies like Landover and Gantly are not creditors. If a customer has an appropriate line of credit and access to payment, we'll make the sale. We leave loans to the experts, and that's certainly not us."

"If the payments were bad enough with the smaller deal you proposed then I wonder what made him go with the bigger deal. Something doesn't sound right to me. I've got to talk to Dad about this, if just for my own benefit. He keeps telling me he's going to teach me how to track our finances. Maybe now is a good time to start."

"It'll certainly introduce you to a wide range of topics; just wish I knew what to do to help."

"I've noticed Dad's attitude has changed since the purchase, and if you hadn't stopped by today, I wouldn't have thought anything about it. He's been awfully nervous about the recent, unseasonably bad weather. When it rains and we can't work, he just stands at his office window and stares out at the clouds, like he's angry at them."

"Your dad never talked to you about any of this?"

"Oh no. Not my father. He keeps everything to himself. I've tried to get him to open up before, but he's just too proud. He would rather die than to let me know he was in trouble. Besides, he's a very hard man to talk to, as you've found out. When he senses a conversation is taking a direction he doesn't like, he simply walks out of the room."

"Like you said, this may be just the opportunity you need to get him to open up a little bit. Hopefully this will turn out to be an exercise in paranoia, but it won't hurt to ask."

"Dad's leaving this afternoon to take a few days off. Maybe I'll talk to him when he gets back. I don't want to spoil his vacation."

"How did you get him to finally take a vacation?"

"It was my mother," Daniel said, smiling. "He worships the ground she walks on. When she says they need to get away, then they get away, though he seemed to be very agreeable about this trip. She seems to be the only one who can get through to him."

"Where are they going?"

"They're driving down to Houston for a few days to visit family in the area."

"Will they be staying in a hotel?"

"No, they'll be staying with my Uncle Tony, Dad's oldest brother, who's also our insurance agent. Dad felt it was something he needed to do this year, since you never know when you will see some people for the last time."

"Life is short, indeed. Make sure you get with him when he gets back." Tom pointed his finger at Daniel and gave him a stern look. "Promise me you will."

"I promise."

"I guess I need to get going before Albert gets back. I don't want to spoil his vacation either. It's probably a good thing I didn't catch him today." The two men stood, and Tom felt a few pains shoot down his lower back. He tried to discreetly stretch his muscles while they finished their conversation, which helped a little. "I can see my way out, Daniel. Let me know how it goes with your dad." He made his way back to the lobby and headed out, anxious to get to his comfortable car seat.

Chapter 8

Late Monday morning, Jack went to the production department to get an update on one of his projects. He found the production manager at the front of the shop looking over his shop area. "Good morning, Glen. I just thought I'd come down here and check on my Stanford Industrial job. We still owe them the last half of their order and I was hoping it would still be going out today."

"We're right on schedule with this order. In fact, we're trying to get it all out by midafternoon. We've got the smaller machine sitting outside, and the freight carrier should be here for it any minute. I've got the larger machine here in the shop so Larry can show the new guy, Pete, how to mount the upper frame, as part of his training. As soon as their done, we'll get it moved outside to wait on the freight carrier, which should be here at about two O'clock. Everything should be on its way to the customer by four."

"You think you got some room in one of the tractors to pack away this box?" he asked, as he handed the box to Glen.

"More sales literature?" Glen asked.

"I got to keep our company name fresh on their minds," Jack responded. Glen put on his safety glasses, walked over to the big machine, and yelled to the men on the scaffolding above, to be heard over the production-shop noise.

"Larry!"

"Yeah, Glen!" Larry responded.

"Everything going okay?"

"I'm just trying to explain to Pete how to properly use the lifting chains to test-fit this framework. We should be done in about thirty minutes."

"Great. We've got trucks scheduled to be here after lunch. Also, I need you to pack this loose box away somewhere," he said, as he raised the box to display it to Larry then set it on the table. Glen walked back over to Jack and removed his safety glasses.

"Sounds good, Glen. They'll be pleased."

As Jack was about to walk away, Jerry came into the shop, fully armed with his clipboard and pen, and donning his safety goggles. "Good morning, Jack, Glen."

"Good morning, Jerry," they both replied.

"Another inspection?" Glen asked.

"Just a casual walk-through, today. It shouldn't take long. Besides, your guys are pretty good about keeping the shop clean and wearing their safety glasses." Before going any further, Jerry raised his clipboard, positioned his pen to write, and whistled as he rocked himself back-and-forth on his heels.

"I guess I'll go call my customer," Jack said, "to let them know their equipment will be shipping out today. It's about a three-hour drive to their yard. They may or may not stay late to receive the order tonight, but at least it'll be there first thing in the morning. Thanks for the extra effort, Glen." Jack's cell phone rang. "Hey, Gary," he answered. "How's it going? I just got your package—" Jack stopped to listen.

"Jerry, I guess I'll leave you to your inspection," Glen said. "I need to get outside and check on that truck." He noticed Jerry had still not moved. "Did you need me for something?" Glen asked, as he slipped on his safety glasses. Jerry stopped rocking.

"Oh, no, Glen," he said with a smile. "I was waiting to see if you were going to put on your safety glasses before you headed out into the production area."

"Wow! You don't miss anything do you? Be careful when you get to the back of the shop. They're cleaning up an oil spill." Jack hung up his cell phone.

"Hey, Glen," Jack called. "I need to take that box back. I forgot some stuff. I'll send it out later through the shipping department or something."

"No problem." Glen grabbed the box and handed it back to Jack. "I'll let Larry know it's not going." Glen headed into the shop, and Jack took the box and headed back to his office.

"How do you get yourself fired over such a simple process, Gary?" Jack whispered to himself while shaking his head. "Good thing I found out before I wasted this package."

Entering the production area, Jerry stopped by the big machine to look it over. He had not seen equipment this size before, which was quite different from the lawn equipment his last employer manufactured. He walked around the front, admiring all the interesting features. Up above, Larry continued his training with Pete.

"This sketch shows some examples of how to rig the overhead crane with lifting chains for loads this size," Larry said.

"I don't understand why we have to use so many different chains," Pete fussed.

"That's where the sketch comes in. You don't have to understand, just follow the layout shown."

"Who made the sketch?"

"Some guys."

"What guys? Just some random guys?"

"Guys that know stuff. You know, engineering kinda guys. They wouldn't let us use it if it wasn't right."

"Can't we just hook it up direct and avoid all this extra work?" Pete questioned.

"I told you, follow the sketches. Besides, I know what I'm

doing. This is fifteen years of experience talking, and this is the proper way. Your suggestion would make the lift angle too low."

"Lift angle? What's the lift angle?"

"This is the angle the lifting chain makes with the horizontal." Larry drew a quick sketch to illustrate his explanation.

"But your method seems so complicated. Why does the lift angle matter?"

"Everybody knows you don't go below forty-five degrees!" Larry argued.

"But why?"

Larry spread out his arms as he searched for a response. "Because I said so!"

Unsatisfied with the response, Pete looked below and saw Jerry. "Let's ask Jerry."

"He's not going to know anything about the specifics of lifting heavy equipment. He'll just tell you the same thing I've been trying to explain. The chains have to be at a forty-five-degree angle or more, and that's just the way it is."

"But why? There has to be a reason. They just don't tell you forty-five degrees and not give an explanation as to why. Besides, if it's a safety matter then Jerry should know."

"Look!" Larry briefly closed his eyes. "Fine! We'll ask Jerry!" Larry looked over the scaffolding, down below. "Hey, Jerry!"

"Yeah, this is Jerry," he replied to the unfamiliar face, as he looked up and used his hand to try to shield his eyes from the bright ceiling lights. "How can I help you?"

"My name is Larry, and I'm trying to explain to this new guy, Pete, how to properly use lifting chains. I told him you wouldn't know why, but maybe he'll believe what I've told him about how to use the chains if you tell him the same thing."

"First tell me what you've been instructing him."

"I told him the lift chains must be at a forty-five-degree angle, or more, with the horizontal. Isn't that correct?"

"That's the normal rule of thumb."

Larry gave Pete a quick I-told-you-so look before turning

back to Jerry and outlining the specifics of their lift. "The frame we are lifting has a ninety-two-inch lift-eye spread and the chains currently on the crane have a total horizontal spread capability of ninety-six inches. He thinks that since the chains will reach the lift eyes that it's okay to use them alone, but I'm saying we need longer chains, and possibly a spreader bar."

"You are correct, Larry. You need to use additional rigging to increase the chain lift angle."

"But why?" Pete hollered, for Jerry to hear.

"You don't have to tell him why, Jerry," Larry countered, "and we don't expect you to know why. Just quote him some chapter, section, and volume number from one of your safety books that says the chains must be at a forty-five-degree angle or more. That'll suffice."

"It's not that simple, Larry," Jerry responded.

"Then, pray tell, what is the answer we seek, oh wise one?" Larry said with a smirk. Jerry rattled off his response with no hesitation.

"With the lengths that Larry has described, Pete, you're making an approximate fifteen-degree angle between the lifting chain and the framework. This small angle imposes a great amount of stress on the chains because of the horizontal force that is reacting along with the vertical force due to the load you're lifting. The vector sum of these two forces combine in the lifting chain and its value is calculated the same way as the hypotenuse on a right triangle. In fact, if you do the calculations for the layout you have, it's about a four-to-one ratio of chain force to lifting force. So, if you're lifting eight-thousand pounds, you are imposing an approximate thirty-two-thousand-pound force on the lifting chain, which probably exceeds its rating. Increasing the lift angle decreases the force on the lifting chain. The forty-five-degree angle Larry mentioned yields an approximate forty-percent increase in chain force versus lifting force, but that can usually be managed. And of course, as the angle increases, the chain force and lifting force approach a one-to-one ratio."

Larry and Pete, both found themselves staring at Jerry with their mouths open, unable to speak, and not blinking their eyes.

"Is there anything else I can do for you?" Jerry offered.

"So, the chains need to be at a forty-five-degree angle or more, right, Jerry?" Pete asked, still mesmerized.

"Basically, yes," he responded.

Larry and Pete looked at each other wide-eyed and spellbound. "You were right, Larry," Pete admitted. "Forty-five degrees or more. No other explanation needed."

"Yeah," Larry responded. "I agree."

"Hey, Larry!" Jerry yelled. Larry looked back over the scaffolding.

"Yeah, Jerry."

"What is this?" Jerry asked, pointing at an object on the table next to him.

"That's an oil filter, Jerry," Larry mocked.

"Oh, okay. Thanks. I'll see you guys around." Jerry walked off, as he continued his inspection.

"Huh," Larry snickered. "These safety guys don't know anything."

"I'll say," Pete agreed.

Tom made it back to the office around 2:00pm. Once inside, he set a few things on his desk then made his way down the hall to see Chris. "Hey, Chris," he said, as he entered his office. Chris continued to type on his laptop as he responded to the familiar voice.

"Come on in Tom and have a seat."

"I can come back later if you're busy."

"Oh, no. I'm just finishing a proposal. I'll be through in a few seconds." He finished his typing as Tom sat down. "There. It's saved and ready to go." He turned his chair around to face his desk and stretched out his arms and fingers. "Typing was never my favorite thing. How's your day going?"

"Great. It was good to be out of the office this morning. I was a little apprehensive to come back and face Jonathan so soon but was pleasantly surprised to not see his car in the parking lot."

"He left for lunch around 11:30 and hasn't been back since. I think he had a doctor's appointment. Anything exciting happen today?"

"I finally made some headway with that customer out in Haslet, Torres Construction. This is the one I told you we lost to Landover about four months ago, just out of the blue."

"Oh yeah, I remember that one. It's a good thing you didn't jump the gun and spend the sales commission early."

"You're telling me."

"Did you learn anything new about the deal?"

"Not yet, but I'm hoping I will soon. Landover has done the same thing to us on several deals over the last eighteen months or so, but I can't figure out if they're just lowering their price at the last minute or what. And if they're just lowering their price, why would customers even give them a last-minute opportunity, especially like this deal, after they gave us full assurance we would be the supplier?"

"I guess until customers actually release a purchase order to a specific supplier, they can pretty much do whatever they want, no matter how unethical it may appear."

"I know, but it doesn't make me feel any better. At least when the competition lowers their price they're making less profit, and on this deal, I went in very tight, so they couldn't have made much. Besides, they can't do that forever, though we know Charles has tried the same thing around here for quite a while."

"Hopefully it is price and not something worse."

"You mean like something under the table?" Tom asked.

"As you know, purchasing agents often go unchecked by their employers as long as everything appears to be on the up-and-up. Their position gives them a lot of power to make all kinds of decisions and, being human, just makes them more susceptible to temptation."

"But Torres Construction doesn't have a purchasing agent, so the owner signs off on all purchases of this magnitude. It had to be price."

"There has been many a man talked into something he didn't want to do by a silver-tongued salesman. Trust me." He reached out his arm to Tom. "This watch was given to me by the guy who sold me my last new car about four years ago. I knew the payments would be tough for a while and actually wanted something less expensive, but he pushed all the right buttons and pumped up my pride to the point that I bought the car just to show him I could. The free watch sealed the deal." Chris snickered. "And to make it worse, if I had bought a less expensive car, I could have easily bought the watch myself, and they'd both be paid for by now. Even after I came to work here, I was still quite bitter about the deal. But since you introduced me to Christ, I've been able to put it behind me." He looked at his watch. "Just four more payments and it's all mine."

"Temptation can be a very strong force, and none of us are immune to it."

"I wonder if I would have given into that guy had I been a Christian at the time."

"You'll never know, but at least you could have prayed about it before making a hasty decision."

"You're right. God would have probably shown me a way out of it."

Tom thought for a moment. "As much as I hate to admit it, the situation with Torres Construction may be something similar to your experience. After all, how could Landover sell them five pieces of equipment when, as far as I could tell, they could barely afford the four pieces we had quoted? Maybe Daniel can help me learn something from this experience."

"Daniel?"

"Albert's son. He's the best mechanic they've ever had but

still pretty green when it comes to the business side, though he's trying awfully hard to learn. Guns and engines are his forte."

"Guns?"

"Excellent marksman. He competes in several tournaments a year. He's won his share of medals and ribbons." Tom noticed a still silence in the office. "Are you holding the fort down by yourself? I didn't see Richard's car outside."

Chris snickered. "He was so worried last week that the credit department was going to axe his sale to Southerland Works. He found out this morning all they needed was a copy of their tax-exemption certificate, and everything was fine. Once he got that taken care of, he left about one O'clock to go celebrate."

"Maybe that will silence his credit-department conspiracy."

They looked at each other with inquisitive stares. "Nah!" they said in unison.

"Your office looks like you've been busy today," Tom noted.

"The phones have been active all day. At least Richard stayed long enough for them to slow down. I've had calls from all over north Texas and got a good lead for a SG1280 to a new potential customer in Gainesville. That's who I was typing the proposal for when you came in."

"Speaking of proposals, I need to go type up a couple from my morning visits, so I better get at it." Tom stood to leave.

"Anything big?"

"Just a couple of small machines like the one you're quoting."

"They may be small, but enough of them add up."

"That's true," Tom agreed, as he made his way to his office.

Wentworth Drilling was a long haul from Landover, further than most of Jack's competition was willing to drive, which shrunk the field of potential suppliers. The account had been fruitful for Jack in the past and, bent on winning their latest quotation, he was not about to endure these long drives for nothing.

He sat in the spacious lobby going over his hand-written notes while waiting for Gordon's production meeting to end. Hearing a sudden increase of conversational noise, Jack gathered his things just as he noticed Gordon entering the lobby, carrying a few loose folders. "Good afternoon, Jack," he greeted. "Come on back." Jack followed him down the short hallway and when they reached his office Gordon stood to the side as he welcomed Jack in. "Come on in, Jack, and have a seat." Jack entered Gordon's office and stood at his desk, scanning the well-organized desktop for any useful information he might uncover before taking his seat. Gordon made his way around his desk and put away the loose folders before sitting down, which gave Jack a little more time to notice all the proposals displayed on Gordon's desk—his on top—but all the competitive pricing was covered by a wooden ruler.

It could be worse, Jack thought. *All I have to do is get him to measure something.* He smiled.

"What brings you all the way out here today?"

"I wanted to come by to be sure you got my proposal for your latest equipment need."

"I've got yours, along with a few others, and was just going over all of them to help our operations manager make his choice."

"There's no need to look at anyone else," Jack kidded. "You know Landover is the best choice for you—take my word for it."

"I've got to do something to keep you honest, Jack," Gordon quipped.

"How do we look, so far?"

"It looks like everyone is in the same ballpark in regard to pricing, but you know our manager is very fond of Chancellor Equipment, just down the road, so it's going to be a tough sale for anyone else."

"Sure, Gordon, but we've been in this situation before and we've always been able to make it work, you and me. I'm sure once you do the comparative analysis, you'll see we offer the best solution to your need."

"That may be, Jack, but Mr. Sullivan is going to expect more than a salesman's pitch this go-around."

"Is there anything you've seen so far that would limit our chances: technical specifications, operational features, pricing…"

"I was comparing the different offerings earlier this morning." Gordon pulled out the various equipment specification sheets from behind their respective quotations. Jack glued his eyes to the wooden ruler, wishing he could will it to move as Gordon rummaged through the paperwork. To his amazement and disappointment, Gordon was able to remove the documents without disturbing the ruler. "Here is what I've been comparing." Gordon turned the documents around and lined them up across his desk for Jack to see, as he used a pencil to point to specific line items of interest. "There are only four bids, so it's not hard to do a quick side-by-side comparison. Here, you can see the horsepower of your tractor is about seven less than the one from Chancellor, but more than the other two. Also, the reach on your tractor is about nine inches shorter than Chancellor's but longer than the other two."

Jack could see where this was headed, as he interjected his own summation. "Looking at all the features listed, it looks like we're in a runoff with Chancellor." *Though it's more of a petty squabble*, he thought.

"That's the conclusion I've come to. Both of you offer the features and optional accessories we need and are competitively priced, which is why I said this one will be a hard sale for you, given Mr. Sullivan's preference." Gordon drew his arms back from across his desk to lean back in his chair, accidently bumping the ruler, which he promptly moved back, but it exposed Chancellor's price long enough for Jack's keen sales eye to catch it. He calculated a rough mental comparison.

Fifteen-hundred dollars, he thought. *That is not a lot of money for a sale this big.* "How is the tractor working that you bought from us last year? It's the same model as the one we have quoted for this job."

"As far as I know, it's working great. We haven't had any trouble with it."

"Are there any features on the Chancellor tractor that you feel would have benefited our tractor, to have done a better job for you?"

"Probably not, but Mr. Sullivan is looking at everything: price, performance, service. Again, Chancellor is just down the road and you guys are one-to-two hours away to get a technician up here, and that's if you have someone immediately available."

Jack thought for a moment. *It looks like he's going to make this one a little harder than the last sale. It's either price or something else.* "Would it make your decision any easier if I told you we are running a special this week, offering an eighteen-hundred-dollar discount on this tractor?"

"I'm not sure if that alone would swing the deal, Jack."

Jack smiled. *Now I know where he's headed.* "Maybe I should go back to the office, sharpen my pencil, and see if there is anything I forgot to supply."

"Yes. Maybe there is an option or accessory that could enhance your proposal to make it a better fit for us." Gordon smiled.

Jack gathered his things and prepared to leave. "Great, Gordon. I guess I've got some homework to do. By the way," he said, "do you have any gift suggestions for a good business associate that is hard to buy for?"

"Is he an electronics enthusiast like me?"

"Now that you mention it, I believe he is."

"Here." Gordon reached for the mailer he had on his desk and handed it to Jack. "Take my copy of the latest sales ad from our local electronics supplier. There may be a couple of things in there your friend would like." Jack took the sales ad, noticed a few items circled with yellow highlighter, and tucked it under his arm. "Oh, and here's one of my new business cards," Gordon added.

Jack examined the new business card. "Nothing has changed, has it?" Then, flipping the card over and noticing Gordon's home address scribbled on the back, "Oh, okay. I just noticed you changed the ...font." *I don't think he would make it as a spy. Why doesn't he just write it on his office wall—bring gift, get purchase order.* "Do you have any idea when you will be releasing this order?"

"It will likely be within the next couple of weeks. I want to give you time to gather information on the accessories you plan on offering so I can more favorably compare you to the competition."

"I'll get to work on this right away and come see you when I have it all together. We can work out the details then, and you'll see I have no competition."

"I'm sure you won't let me down, Jack." Jack gathered his things and left, whistling as he left the building.

"They should all be this easy," Jack said with a smile.

Chapter 9

Daniel started looking for the Landover purchase contract early Tuesday morning. It was not in any of the usual purchasing or supplier folders, but he found it in one of the filing cabinets behind Albert's desk, in a separate folder labeled, My Last Deal. He took the contract to his office and scanned it over, hoping he might recognize something, but nothing looked familiar to him.

Tom was on his way to a cold call in Haltom City when his cell phone rang. "Hello, this is Tom. May I help you?"

"Good morning, Tom, this is Daniel with Torres Construction. When you were here yesterday you mentioned something about the purchase contract for the equipment we bought from Landover. I got curious this morning and hunted it down, which is no small task in our office, given Dad's random folder-naming method. I'm sitting at my desk trying to educate myself on some of the details, but I'm not having much luck. This stuff is all new to me, and I'm really not sure what I'm looking for anyway."

"Those things can be complicated, especially if you're not used to looking at them. Is there anything in particular you're looking for?"

"I thought I would know when I saw it, but nothing sticks out at me. I guess I'm trying to get an idea on the size of the debt and what it's going to cost us."

"That information shouldn't be too hard to find."

"That's why I called you. I figured you had probably seen a million of these things. I was hoping you could coach me a little."

"It would be best if you had someone point that stuff out to you in person. Contracts change between suppliers, and the same information can be located in different places, depending on the contract. If you would like, I could come by sometime today, after lunch, and give you a hand."

"Better yet, if you're willing to come out here, I'll meet you somewhere halfway for lunch, and you can have one on me."

"Sure, that's not a problem. Let's meet at that place in Saginaw, Randall's, at about 11:45. We both seem to like that place."

"Will do, Tom, and thanks."

"See you then. Oh, Daniel," he added. "See if you can find a copy of the bank loan agreement, too." Tom was anxious to help, but he knew his limitations. *Lord, please give me wisdom.*

Bill's investigation was coming to a head, and he had invited Paul Grissom to his office to discuss his findings. Paul stepped into the doorway of Bill's office and announced himself. "You need to see me?"

"Yes, Paul. Come on in and shut the door behind you." Bill set his sales and service reports aside as Paul took a seat across from Bill's desk. Though company president, Bill's office was not an elaborate showplace. It was spacious, but necessarily so, for all the meetings he convened. He still had his original furniture from before the renovations—mostly for sentimental reasons—which still looked new, though he had splurged on some nice, new office chairs. His wife had done the decorating, adding a few live plants and art prints, and most of the pictures on the walls were of his family. The windows offered a view of the surrounding area, though it was nothing spectacular, but it was the best you could get in the industrial area where their business resided.

"Paul, as you know from our meeting last Friday, we have been carrying out an investigation to try and uncover what appear to be some unscrupulous actions on the part of what we believe to be one individual."

"Do you have any idea who it is?"

"I'm sure it's one of your salesmen, Jack Fisher."

"Jack Fisher?" Paul asked surprised. "Are you positive?"

"I'm fairly certain it is, but I thought it would be wise to get you involved, since you are his supervisor, and get your opinion." Bill opened one of his desk drawers, removed a folder and offered it to Paul. "Take a look at some of these contracts."

Paul opened the folder, which contained six separate purchase contracts, and he began to peruse them one at a time. "Is there something wrong with them? Nothing seems to be out of the ordinary to me."

"Not by themselves." Bill reached into his desk drawer for another folder. "But compare those copies with the ones in this folder." Bill handed Paul the second folder. "This folder contains a copy of each of the six contracts you have. From a casual glance, each set of copies appears to be exact duplicates. But when you read them closely you will notice the special instructions between each respective copy are different."

Paul began comparing the contracts. "I don't understand. Why do we have two different copies of the same contract, and where did the different copies come from?"

"The first set of documents I gave you has our standard special instructions and is what we have on file here at the office as official contracts. The second set of contracts is bogus, having been modified after-the-fact. We learned about them through the service department from customers who have come in over the last several months for the free services we have promised them, as outlined in their respective special instructions. Each time someone has come in with a doctored contract we've asked for a copy of it, which they have all obliged to give us. My theory is that the salesman has used these tactics to get the equipment business, which in and of itself is not a problem—it's the hiding of it and the illegal contract editing that concerns me. There appears to be more to this than what is obvious. Why wouldn't a salesman just come out and make these conditions part of the contract and let everybody know about it? After all, we've given away free service before as part of a sale."

"It looks like there are only three customers involved."

"That we know of," Bill added. "These are just the ones that have come to light in recent months. I'm sure there will be more."

"One of the customers has three contracts in your stack, one has two, and the last, Beckett Construction, has only one. Do you think the customers are doctoring the contracts themselves?"

"I suppose that's possible," Bill admitted, "but surely, they would know we have the original copy on file. Besides, I have additional evidence." Bill reached behind his desk and pulled a packed file folder from the floor. "I've had Walter trace all of Jack's credit card and reimbursable expenses for the last year, and he has uncovered some disturbing facts. This folder is a culmination of Walter's efforts covering this same time period, chock full of credit card receipts and shipping documents. It appears there have been many purchases over the last year or so for things shipped to several of Jack's customers, including two of the three customers represented by this stack of contracts. To be fair, we've made the same analysis for all the salesmen, but no suspicious transactions surfaced for anyone else."

"From a quick glance, the purchases don't seem to be too unusual, Bill. As you know, all our salesmen buy thank-you gifts for their customers."

"Walter has compared the dates of all these purchases with the dates the respective contracts were released and found that many times these were gifts for perspective buys, not thank-you gifts for contracts we had won. In fact, some of these gifts went to customers we eventually lost the bid with; apparently as an attempt, or enticement, to sway the purchasing agent to reconsider his decision of releasing a contract to the competition. I bet if the shipments could be traced far enough, we'd learn that these gifts are benefiting the purchasing agents more than the companies they work for."

"I guess I've gotten a little lax in reviewing his credit card statements," Paul admitted. "I had no idea this was going on."

"Don't be too hard on yourself, Paul. The big increase in sales over the last two years has caught us all by surprise, making these expenses seem almost normal, certainly acceptable, for the revenue generated. Besides, without a thorough analysis it would have been impossible to match these purchases with specific contracts and order dates; and who knows whether he's been using his own personal credit card for more intimate or expensive thank-yous. Overall, this kind of activity borders on reciprocity and is luring customers to purchase from us under false pretenses, almost like a bribe, something we have never condoned. We sell our reputation, not our souls!"

"Based on what you've uncovered so far, what can we do now?"

"Right now, I just want you to be aware of what we see going on. Keep a close eye on Jack and let me know if you notice any unusual activity with him. You might even try to get involved with some of his customers to see if you can identify anything amiss with their relationships."

"Do you think we need to confront Jack on this?"

"Certainly, we do, and we will, but I think we need just a little more time. I'm going to make a few more phone calls to investigate these contracts a little deeper. I learned today that one of our customers fired their purchasing agent yesterday for accepting gifts like this. Maybe other customers will be willing to shed some light on what's going on if they are aware. Even if customers are doctoring their own contracts, it doesn't explain the untimely credit card purchases."

Paul handed all the paperwork back to Bill. "I'll certainly keep an eye on him and let you know if I notice anything out of line. Just let me know when you want to talk with him, and we can get this taken care of."

"To be honest with you, Paul, if this turns out to be only half as bad as it seems, I will probably insist that you fire Jack. You might consider looking for another salesman."

"I thought as much," Paul said. "I can take care of that. I'll put the word out to our headhunters by the end of the day."

"And do it discretely. We don't want to scare Jack off before we get to the bottom of this. If nothing else, I'd like to give him a chance to explain himself. It won't make right what he's done, but it may make him think twice before he does it again someplace else."

"Sure thing. I'll get right on it."

Paul left Bill's office and headed down the hallway. Finding Jack in, he knocked on his door to announce himself. "Anybody home?"

"Come on in, Paul. I was just writing up a few proposals."

Paul approached Jack's desk and took a seat across from him. He reached for the electronics retailer's sales ad from Jack's desk. "That's a long drive for a flat screen TV, isn't it?"

Jack turned around and noticed Paul holding the ad. *Uh oh.* "Oh, that old thing?" *Remain calm. It's for the better.* "It came as stuffing in a package I received. I saw a few good deals, and was going to throw it out, but thought I might at least compare their prices with some local suppliers."

Paul thumbed through the pages. "I didn't think you liked Mac computers," he said, noticing one of the selections.

"People can change, can't they, Paul?" he said smiling. "Their mind, I mean."

"Sure, Jack. Just sometimes, it's a total surprise." He tossed the ad back onto Jack's desk. "Just when you think you know a guy, right?" Paul smiled. "By the way, I just remembered I never asked you how your meeting went last Friday."

"Meeting?"

"Your lunch meeting; you know, with the new, potential client."

He raised his eyebrows. *Why now?* "Oh yeah, the lunch meeting."

"Is the company from around here?"

Remember, it's not wrong if it's for your good. "He wasn't really clear on any details. I think they're from out of town."

"Did he give you a company name?"

What's next, bright lights and bamboo under my fingernails? "I got the feeling he wasn't comfortable with disclosing too much information at this time, so I didn't press him too hard for any. You know the drill," Jack said, as he sensed his shoulders tighten and his body getting stiffer.

"He must be one cool customer. What's his name?"

Again, the questions! I need more time to think. "Name?"

"He does have a name, doesn't he?"

"Of course, he does," Jack said smiling. "I just can't remember it right now. In fact, I was just looking for his contact information when you came in." Jack glanced around his office, to his left, then right, and shuffled a few papers on his desk. "I know it's here somewhere, and I'll find it before I have to call him back."

"Do you think anything will come out of the meeting?"

"As it turns out, the guy is interested in one of our machines."

"Great! Which one?"

"It's hard to say at this time. I'm still evaluating his need and what I, uh, we have to offer to meet that need."

"Sounds like it was a profitable meeting. Any idea on when he'll make a decision?"

"He's really waiting on an answer from me, that is, you know, to offer the proper model. I've got about two weeks to decide."

"Great! Looks like your year just continues to get better, doesn't it?"

"My year?" Jack asked with a straight face.

"Your sales figures. They just continue to get better, don't they?"

"Oh yeah, my sales figures! What can I say? I've been given the best opportunity to learn by working with you guys …and stuff." *That was a lame line.*

Paul snickered. "I guess it's best we helped your sales figures, because it doesn't sound like we've helped you any with your grammar. Anything else on the horizon?"

"Not really. Just the usual stuff."

"As you know, the usual stuff is just as important as anything else. It's often the usual stuff that gets us in trouble, too. Right?" Jack just nodded his head, as Paul stood. "I better get back to my office. I have a thousand things to get done. I just wanted to let you know I didn't forget about your meeting."

"Thanks for asking, and I appreciate your support." Jack sat rigid until Paul left his office. "Whew," he whispered as he relaxed his body and dropped his shoulders. "That felt awful weird. I think I need to take a drive."

Jack was relieved to get out of the office, or was it away from Paul, or away from guilt. *Guilt? I don't have any guilt!* he told himself. *I just need more time to consider my options. Besides, Gantly may not be my choice. I like the way things are going now, but I need Paul to stay out of this one.*

He drove around for about half an hour, with no specific destination in mind, ending up at an office building still under construction, where he knew Warren was working. Familiar with construction-site protocol, he donned his hard hat and safety glasses, and entered the complex, weaving through construction workers toting raw materials and power tools, looking for his friend. Thankfully, most of the heavy construction work was completed, so the noise level inside was reduced—though not enough for someone accustomed to an office environment—to the constant sawing, hammering, and drilling of wall panels and trim work.

"Jack!" Warren hollered, from one of the side rooms. Jack spotted the familiar face and made his way over. "You just wanted to see how real men work, didn't you?" he kidded. Jack rolled his eyes with a smile. "Come in here," he directed. "All the sheetrock is hung in this area, and it makes it a little quieter." They entered the room, and Warren closed the door behind them, which was a relief to Jack's ears. "So, what brings you out here today?"

"I was in the area and thought I'd pay you a visit. It's been a while since I've been to one of your job sites."

"I think the last one was that medical place over on Miner Boulevard. We helped with their food-services renovation."

"Oh yes," Jack said, throwing his head back. "What a crazy place that was. I'll never go back there for anything."

"Never say never, Jack. I'm sure if you needed medical attention bad enough, and it was close by, you'd go."

"Not me," he said. "That's the beauty of life, Warren; it's full of choices, and I choose to not go there."

"Things change, Jack."

"Only if you let them," he insisted, "and I choose when I want change. But your work there was excellent, as always."

"What do you think of this job?" Warren asked, as he spread out his hands and directed Jack's attention to the walls around them, in their various stages of completion.

Jack glanced around the room, not noticing anything in particular. "I don't see how you do it, Warren. The same thing over and over again—paint this wall, paint that wall. It would drive me crazy."

"There's more to it than that, Jack."

"I'm sorry, Warren! I didn't mean anything by it. You're great at what you do, and your customers love your work. I'm just saying this may be a perfect fit for you, and it has obviously been very good to you, but it's certainly not for me."

"It's okay, Jack. I love what I do, and it brings me a lot of satisfaction to help transform places like this. Besides, you've got your niche, too, and I know I don't want any part of that."

Jack forced a smile. *Not sure if I want my own niche, at the moment,* Jack thought.

"By the way, have you made up your mind yet about that new job offer? I remember you had to make a decision soon."

"Oh, I have plenty of time; at least another week," he said, *assuming Paul doesn't get any nosier.* "I'm still weighing my options, wanting to get the best deal …for my family, of course."

"Talking about being in demand, Jack, it seems you have everything going your way. Maybe a change is just what you need."

"Maybe," he said, as his cell phone rang. He looked to see it was Paul. "Maybe you're right. I better go, Warren, it's my boss." Jack started out the door.

"You can take your call in here if you would like, where it's quieter."

"I'll see you, Warren." Jack continued his way out the door as he answered his phone. "Hey, Paul," he almost yelled. He paused as he pretended to try to listen. "I can barely hear you. I'll try to call you back after I leave this construction site." He hung up his phone and continued out to his car. "This is getting a little creepy."

Chapter 10

Randall's was a great place to eat, and Tom came here more often than any of the other local restaurants when he was in the area. It was a rustic looking establishment with mostly wooden furnishings, which offered reasonable dining comfort. Like most smokehouses of this type, daily cleaning could remove only so much of the grease, but the guests came for the generous portions of good food, not ambiance.

Tom arrived first and waited in his car for Daniel. It was still a little early before the large lunch crowd began to gather, so he was able to park close to the front. Daniel arrived just a few minutes later, and they both exited their vehicles and approached the restaurant entrance. "Good to see you again, Daniel," Tom said.

"I really appreciate you taking time to help me with this."

"I haven't helped you yet," he cautioned, "but I'll do what I can. Let's get something to eat, and then we'll talk."

The two walked inside and made their way through the short line, selecting their choice of smoked meats and steamy vegetables, and Tom was sure to get some of that buttery-sweet peach cobbler he loved so much. Daniel picked up the tab, as he had offered, despite Tom's polite attempt at the cash register to intervene. Selecting a place in the back corner of the room, hoping it would be more private, they set their trays on the table, situated all their dishes, and got settled in their seats.

When Tom bowed his head to pray, Daniel reached over and grazed Tom's shoulder. "Uh, Tom, would you please pray for me, too?"

"Of course." Tom bowed his head and prayed out loud, as Daniel fumbled with his napkin and left his eyes open, looking around to see if anyone was watching them. Tom ignored the clanging of the silverware and the squeaking of the table from Daniel bouncing his legs. He finished his prayer and noticed Daniel was using his hands like sun visors to shield his eyes from the other patrons, unaware the prayer was over. "Amen," Tom said again, trying to not be obvious. Daniel pulled his head up.

"Thanks, Tom. I need all the help I can get. This deal has got me on pins and needles, and I'm not sure how it's going to turn out." Then, looking down at the smoked ribs on his plate, "Now, this, I can handle."

"I never get disappointed when I come here. I can already feel my taste buds salivating." Tom dug in, and they both ate as they talked. "Did you have anything planned for this weekend?" Tom asked.

"I've got a handgun competition Saturday afternoon."

"That sounds like fun. Is your dad going with you?"

"Not this time, but I'm still working on him. He's hunted with rifles all his life, but finally got interested in learning to shoot handguns just recently, so I've been teaching him for a couple of weeks. For now, he just wants to learn how to hold the gun and shoot. He's not concerned about accuracy at this point."

"It'll take practice, but I'm sure he'll be a crack shot in no time with you as his teacher."

"I'm hoping he'll get interested in competing, or at least going to my tournaments. You got anything planned?"

"Saturday, I'll probably have to mow my yard again. It's

getting to be that time of year when the grass has to be mowed every week."

"I know what you mean. I still go over to my parents' house on most Saturdays to help with their yard work."

"Sunday, we'll be going to church. We have a missionary family from Peru visiting in the morning service. They'll be telling us about the people of Peru and what they're doing to reach them for Christ. I wish you would come and hear their presentation."

"You never know, Tom. You've been after me for quite a while. I guess I should visit at least once."

"And this Sunday would be a great opportunity."

"I don't know," he said. "We'll see."

"Think about it. If it would make you feel more comfortable, bring your mom and dad with you. We'd love to have all of you there." Tom sensed Daniel was a little uncomfortable. "Did your parents make it to Houston without any problems?"

"My mom called last night. They got to my uncle's house okay. They probably won't call again until they get ready to leave Wednesday evening."

"Hopefully, they're having a good time."

"My dad said this will be their last vacation for a long time, so I hope it's a good one."

Having finished most of his lunch, Tom swallowed what he was chewing and wiped his mouth. "Man, that's good stuff. So, how can I help you with your documents?"

"I brought a copy of the purchase contract and the loan agreement as you suggested and was hoping you could look them over and give me some pointers."

"Great," Tom said, as he took another bite.

Daniel reached into his shirt pocket and retrieved the copies. He unfolded them on the table, with the purchase contract on top, turning them to be right-side up for Tom to read. They both kept eating while Tom perused the purchase contract. "For the most part, Daniel," Tom said, finishing his swallow and wiping his mouth, "the purchase contract looks pretty standard, but pay attention to the special terms and conditions here at the bottom." Tom turned the contract around so Daniel could follow along as he began to point out the finer details. "As you can see here, your company was required to submit a twenty percent down payment when the order was placed, and that down payment was non-refundable. Non-refundable down payments are becoming quite common in today's market, so that's nothing to be alarmed about. Twenty percent would have been a substantial amount of money for an order this size. In fact, from the conversations I've had with Albert, this may have been most of, if not all, the cash you guys had available to you, unless Albert took out his loan early."

Setting the purchase contract aside, Tom scanned over the loan papers, looking for the closing date. When he found it, he turned the papers around for Daniel to see and pointed it out to him. "Here, the loan is dated about a month ago, which would have been when your final payment to Landover was due. In my opinion, this would have been the normal sequence for anyone to pay for a purchase like yours. One, you secure a line of credit so it will be available when you need it; two, take receipt of the merchandise; three, wait as long as you can before your final payment is due; then, four, close your loan and pay your debt. This way you don't have to start your loan payments until it is absolutely necessary, assuming you have the cash to make the down payment on the equipment and for the loan. One of the drawbacks is you never know what interest rate you'll be paying until you close unless you get locked in early. And interest rates have been going up in recent months."

Confident that Daniel had taken in all he had just said, Tom spun the loan contract back around to review the loan terms. After a few moments of intense scrutiny, he again turned the papers around and pointed them out to Daniel. "Here, you see your dad was able to put down only five percent of the loan, probably because of the twenty percent he had to put down with

Landover, and that's one reason for the double-digit interest rate you see here. Over in this box you see what the monthly payments are, and this is the length of the loan. I'll bet if you ask your dad, this is going to be one tough loan for you guys to pay back." Daniel just stared at the contract. "Down here," Tom pointed, "it states that your first loan installment is due thirty days after the close of the loan, which was about a week ago. Do you know whether that has been paid or not?"

"Man, I don't know. Dad handles all the big money stuff, and he doesn't share that with anyone, not even mom. I'm sure he made the payment. Otherwise, why would he take a few days off and go out of town?"

"Maybe you're right," Tom said. "Surely, he wouldn't go out of town and spend money he doesn't have. But at any rate, maybe you should get with your dad after his vacation and ask him to explain the contract to you, at least to help you learn more about the business."

"But I'm not sure how to start the conversation."

"He doesn't mind you asking about the business, does he?"

"Oh no. In fact, he encourages me to learn as much as I can, so he won't be upset with me looking over these papers. He's given me full access to all our records and files, customer contracts, and all that stuff; he just doesn't want me going through the check book yet until he thinks I'm ready."

"It sounds like you just need to express your concerns, as I'm sure he has some, too. Unless he has a stash of money put back somewhere, these next few years are going to be financially brutal for you guys. In my opinion, your business is going to have to experience a dramatic increase, almost two-fold, to make ends meet."

"I don't think there's any way that's going to happen," Daniel said. "Maybe my dad just got in too far over his head on this deal."

"Apparently, neither you nor I can answer that question with any certainty. We both have to speculate on this deal, because your dad is the only one who knows the true financial condition of your company. I do know the picture I've painted can't be too much brighter, as I'm sure your dad was very open with me about his finances during our negotiations." Tom thought for a moment. "If your dad is in over his head, there still may a way out of this, but it's a long shot." Daniel's ears perked up and his eyes widened. "You could try selling the larger piece of equipment then refinance your loan. You'll probably have to take a loss on it, but at least it will reduce your debt and your loan payment substantially."

"Do you think Landover will take it back?"

"I doubt that will happen. I know it sounds like a simple solution, but it just isn't realistic. Our companies are not into handling a lot of used equipment, and I believe I speak for both, Landover and Gantly. We may take in a piece of machinery occasionally for a trade-in, but it's always something we know we can quickly turn and get rid of. It would be best if you could find a buyer yourself. There isn't a huge demand for the larger machine you purchased, but they do sell occasionally, so there's probably a buyer for it out there somewhere."

Daniel sat perplexed. "Do you think the situation is that dire, Tom?"

"Only your dad can answer that question." Tom sat back in his seat. "Look, maybe I'm throwing up red flags unnecessarily. I hope all we've been doing is wasting time talking about problems that don't really exist. It will certainly do us no good to fret over this in the meantime."

"Man, this is going to be bad. Either way, my dad is going to be hurt. If I confront him, he'll think I don't trust him. If I do nothing, I'm afraid my dad would rather be destroyed than embarrassed by selling off equipment or postponing raises again just to get by. If your original deal for four pieces of equipment was what my dad wanted in the beginning, why do you think he decided to buy the extra piece? And why suddenly switch to Landover?"

"Daniel, I can't tell you what was in your father's mind when he made the deal with Jack, uh …, Landover."

"Jack? Who's Jack?" Daniel scanned over the purchase contract and spotted Jack Fisher's name at the bottom. "I know him," he said, pointing at his name. "He's the Landover salesman that comes by our shop—the one that made this deal with Dad. Maybe he'll have some answers."

"Slow down, Daniel. First, I suggest you get with your dad and see what he can tell you. Again, all our overreacting may be unwarranted."

"Alright," Daniel agreed. "I'll get with Dad when he comes in Thursday."

"Now let's quit worrying for a while and finish our lunch. My peach cobbler is getting cold."

By the afternoon, the phones had slowed down enough to allow Cheryl to get caught up with auditing some service and sales work-order folders for proper documentation and order of contents. Though the task often got monotonous, there was the seemingly constant running around the office looking for misplaced forms, and it beat staring at a silent telephone during non-peak hours. She stored the folders in boxes, on a table against the wall behind her, which required she turn her back to the lobby while filing, but she kept her ears open in case someone came through the front doors.

The service folders were easier to reconcile, so she started with them, and was finished in less than an hour. Due to their larger dollar amounts and more complex legal procedures, the sales folders required much more effort and focus. She had been staring at the contents of the folder in her hand for several minutes, trying to mentally piece the paper trail together, and something was missing. She counted the purchase orders twice and compared them to their respective journal entries, and all seemed to be in order. All the costs for parts and labor were as estimated, but the overall gross profit was lower than anticipated. She continued to scan the price estimate page when she realized, "That's it," she said, as she slapped the page. "We still need to file for—"

"Cheryl," the deep, gruff, booming voice sounded from the receptionist's counter. Startled, Cheryl turned as she dropped the folder she was holding, to see the unannounced guest. She relaxed her shoulders and stared at the familiar figure.

"Carl, you know not to sneak up on me like that."

"Sorry, Cheryl. I just got back from vacation today, and I haven't had a chance to say hi yet." Cheryl stooped down to pick up the dropped folder and its contents. "You need some help with that?"

"I got it. It isn't a large folder," then looking back at Carl, "but it could've been." She collected all the documents, laid the folder on her desk, and took a seat. "So, how was your vacation?"

"It was real good. Me and my best friend, Willie, went to the west coast for a couple of weeks. We each got friends out there and we wanted to see what all the hoopla was about California. It was a lot of fun, but I'm glad to be back. I had to take yesterday off, too, because my flight back on Sunday got canceled."

"Hey, Cheryl," Jerry called out as he approached the receptionist's desk.

"Jerry, have you met Carl?"

"Carl?" Jerry asked.

"This is Carl Hendricks, our maintenance man."

"Carl, it's a pleasure to meet you. I'm Jerry Simpson, the safety director."

"My pleasure, too, Jerry." Carl stared at Jerry's face. "What's wrong with your eyes?"

"Excuse me?" Jerry asked.

"Your eyes. What's wrong with them that you gotta keep'em covered with them big goggles?"

"Oh, I just forget sometimes to take them off. They're my safety goggles and I wear them a lot," he added, as he removed the goggles and put them in his pocket. Carl looked over at Cheryl, and she gave an affirmative nod. "Jack has told me a lot about you and that you just got back to work yesterday from vacation, but I guess we've been missing each other."

"Actually," Cheryl interjected, "Carl's return flight got canceled until Monday morning, so he didn't get back to work until today."

"And I been busy all mornin' in my maintenance shop tryin' to fix a few things that got put on my workbench while I was gone. I barely took a lunch break. In fact, this is the first chance I've had to come up here and say hi to my girl."

"Your girl?" he asked with a forced smile.

"Cheryl, my young lady friend here."

"Oh, he's just going on. He's always kidding with me," Cheryl responded.

"Oh, I see. Like brother and sister."

Carl stared at Jerry with a smile and replied, "Or maybe not quite so kin." He winked with a click of his tongue.

Jerry clasped his hands together in front of him and extended his index fingers together, pointing at Carl. "Uh, Carl, can I speak with you for just a moment, please?"

"Sure, Jerry, go right ahead."

"In private please? Just for a moment. It will only take a moment."

Carl glanced at Cheryl. "Excuse us darlin'." He and Jerry walked a few paces away from the receptionist's desk and Cheryl went back to her filing. "Yeah, Jerry. How can I help you?"

"Jack said you and I may be able to help each other."

"You mean like, some days you'd do maintenance, and I'd do your safety stuff?" Carl snickered. "I don't think that would work. You see, you can ask most anybody around here; I'm not exactly the shinin' example of safety, if you know what I mean." He showed Jerry the scar on the tip of his left pinky. "Never saw where you can't see." Then, showing Jerry his left thumb, "Never saw too far where you can see." Carl turned his left side toward Jerry and stooped down a little. "And if you look on the back of my right ear—"

"I mean outside of work."

Carl straightened up as he thought for a moment. "I suppose I could help you work on your house, but what is it you could do for me?" He sharpened his eyes. "You're not a gardener, are you? I'd like to grow some good pickles this year."

"I'm not a fulltime gardener, but I know a few things. Besides, you don't grow pickles, you …never mind. You see, Jack thought, since you and I are both single, that we could encourage each other in our respective search for a mate by spending time together."

Carl hesitated for a second. "You mean like therapy?"

"I suppose you could look at it that way. I prefer to think of it as just being there for each other."

Carl gave Jerry a perplexed look. "Now look, Jerry, if you just wanna hang out sometime and go do somethin' together, that's one thing. But when you go to talkin' all touchy feely, that sounds like what girls do."

"For example, let's say you find a girl."

"Like Cheryl?"

"A girl that you like."

"Like Cheryl!"

"You can use her as an example, but it could be any girl."

"Then I'll say Cheryl." Jerry stared at Carl for a moment.

"Okay," he acknowledged, "use Cheryl. Let's say you want an objective opinion of how you two get along with each other, and you just want someone to talk to. You could come over to my place and hang out and watch TV, and we could have an open discussion about what's going on."

"What do you mean by open discussion?"

"Let's say you come over to discuss your acquaintance."

"You mean my girlfriend, right?"

"Sure, your girlfriend."

"So, if we was discussin' me and Cheryl you would give me advice."

"Yes. I would let you know that I don't see any chemistry between you two and, maybe, recommend you find someone more fitting."

"But if it was good chemistry you'd say so, too, right?" Jerry paused for a second.

"Sure, sure, I would."

Carl rubbed his chin as he gave serious thought to the suggestion. "Would you have to meet her?"

"Meet who?"

"My girl! Unless of course, it's Cheryl, and you done met her."

"Not necessarily," Jerry answered.

"Would I have to meet your girlfriend?"

"Not necessarily."

Carl thought again. "I think it could work."

Jerry's eyes widened as he displayed a surprised look. "It could? I mean, yes, it could work. Wow. How odd would it be, if we never meet each other's girlfriend and we end up with the same one?" Jerry joked.

Carl tilted his head. "Now I don't think that's ever gonna happen." Jerry glanced over at Cheryl. "Jerry, it's been good to talk with you, and I look forward to gettin' to know you better. Maybe we can do somethin' this weekend."

"Sure, we'll do something this weekend."

"I gotta run now, but I'll see you around." Carl walked back toward the sales department as Jerry started in the opposite direction.

"Are you going back by Tony's office, Carl?" Cheryl called out.

"I sure am."

"Would you take this folder to him and let him know I was able to reformat his database, and found the problem with his spreadsheet that he e-mailed me yesterday?"

Jerry stopped in his tracks and stood motionless for a moment, staring through a painting hanging on the wall and absent-mindedly rubbing its frame as he eavesdropped on the conversation.

"How about this," Carl replied, "I'll take the folder to Tony, and tell him to call you about the other stuff."

"That'll work. Thanks, Carl." Cheryl looked around and noticed Jerry in the hall. "You like that painting, Jerry?" she asked.

Jerry turned her direction. "Painting? What painting?" Cheryl gestured with her eyes toward the painting. "Oh, this painting," he responded, darting his eyes around the canvas, and touching the frame on both sides.

"Is there something wrong with it?" she asked.

Without turning away, Jerry took a step back and framed the picture between his outstretched arms. "It looks a little crooked," he said, leaning his body right and left, with one eye closed.

"Not again," she said, as she stood up and made her way over to the painting. "The hanger must not be centered correctly." When she arrived, Jerry backed up a few steps to give her room to fully inspect the scene. Cheryl looked the painting over as Jerry got the first whiff of a very familiar fragrance. His eyes lit up.

"Mama?" he whispered.

Cheryl turned around. "Did you say something, Jerry?"

"Mama …mia," he said. "Mama mia, it really is crooked, isn't it?" he said, pointing back at the painting.

Cheryl turned back around to take another look, as Jerry rolled his eyes back, exhaled a sigh of relief. After a short pause, he mustered his courage, closed his eyes, leaned toward her, and sniffed her perfume again. He smiled as he exhaled. Cheryl turned back around just as Jerry had stepped back and opened his eyes. "Crooked!" he said, with a deer-in-the-headlights look.

116

"I told you it was crooked, isn't it?"

"It doesn't look crooked to me," she said with a final examination.

"Oh, okay. My mistake," he rattled off. "I guess I'd better get going. I'll see you around Cheryl." Before Cheryl could respond, he disappeared down the hall.

Chapter 11

"Good morning, Tom," Chris said, as he entered Tom's office and took a seat from across his desk.

"Hey, Chris. Ready to kick off your Wednesday?"

"Got my customers all lined up like dominoes and I'm determined to get a purchase order from every one of them."

"Right," Tom said, as they both laughed. "If it were that easy, we would both be rich."

"No. I'm sure the business world would find a way to restructure commission plans to keep us all on an even keel. So, unless there has been a recent increase in corporate pity for salesmen, I'll be heading north this morning to tout my wares and, hopefully, win another sale. I've got a couple of stops around Gainesville."

"It would have been closer to have left directly from your house," Tom noted.

"I had the same idea but realized this morning I forgot to take my stuff home last night, so, here I am. Speaking of stuff," he said, as he stood, pulled a tape measure from his pocket, and walked over to Tom's coatrack.

"What are you doing?" Tom asked.

"I need some measurements to be sure my coats will fit."

"Do you think this is a good time?"

"It's early," Chris insisted. "I've got a few minutes before Jonathan or Richard shows up."

"I hope so, as I'm sure no one will think it's weird a salesman brought a tape measure to work."

"It would've looked awkward, if not suspicious, had I actually brought my coats in to try them on the rack."

"And this doesn't?"

"It'll just take a second and no one will be the wiser," Chris said, as he began gathering his data. Then, looking back at Tom, "If the tape measure isn't quite stealthy enough for you, I suppose I could use my shoe as a measuring stick; that wouldn't get any second looks, huh!"

"Not from a cobbler," Tom joked.

"Besides," Chris asked, "how accurate would that be?"

"Accurate? No. Harmful to the environment? Yes."

"The old bad-foot-breath humor, huh. It never gets old, Tom," he said, finishing with the coatrack dimensions. "It's not near as bad as it used to be."

"What, my humor?" Tom asked with a smile.

"No, my foot odor. It's gotten better since I started putting baking soda in my shoes at night."

"No doubt a helpful suggestion garnered from one of the many cooking shows you watch on the weekend," Tom kidded. "Got any new spatula tips or cast-iron skillet tricks to share?"

"Wow! Someone is really on their game this morning. You've got a comeback for everything. It's almost like having a conversation with …"

"Hey, guys," Richard called out, as he stepped into the office doorway. Chris turned toward the door, reeled in the tape measure behind him, and slipped it into his back pocket.

"Look, Chris, it's Richard" Tom announced.

"Yes, it is. Before starting time, huh, Richard?"

"I left a little early this morning thinking I needed to get gas, then I remembered I filled up last night. Didn't want to lose the momentum, you know."

"Right," Chris said. "You gotta keep the mojo going, for sure, even if it means getting to work six minutes early," he said, glancing at his watch.

"Early is early," Richard said, as they all laughed. "Admiring that coatrack, are you, Chris?" Chris made an animated gesture of innocence. "Don't blame you. It's a nice looker. Tom, you're not thinking of getting rid of it are you? I'll take it off your hands if you are. I need something to replace my five-gallon bucket of sand with a stick in the middle of it."

"I thought you were using that to grow a ficus tree…and it died," Chris joked.

"It was a ficus tree," Richard responded. "A fake one. After three years of gathering dust, it was easier to cut off the limbs than clean the leaves. It had a beefy trunk, so I put it to work."

"As a coatrack?" Chris asked.

"More like a coat stick," Richard answered. "But it has served its purpose. Just looking for some ideas to modernize the office furniture a little."

"A little?" Chris asked in jest. "Richard, your office furniture consists of a refurbished warehouse desk, two chairs that don't match, a beat-up filing cabinet, and shattered remnants of a ficus tree planted in a bucket of sand. It may take more than a nice coatrack to spruce the place up." They all laughed.

"Admittedly, it's not the Taj Mahal, but I have to start somewhere," Richard answered with a smile.

"How about starting with your office door that doesn't close?" Chris suggested.

"I've been on maintenance to get that taken care of. Thanks for the reminder." Then, turning to Tom, "Now, about that coatrack."

"Not so fast, Richard," Tom replied.

"Just kidding," Richard said. "I know you'd never let it go." He paused, gazing at the coatrack. "How tall is that thing?" he directed to Chris, as he surveyed the assembly.

Chris reached for his tape measure, then caught himself.

120

"How should I know. It's his coatrack," Chris said, pointing to Tom. "I'm just awkwardly standing next to it for no apparent reason, I guess," as he managed to migrate a few steps away.

"What's your best guess?" Richard asked.

"Yeah, Chris, what's your best guess?" Tom added. Chris looked over at Tom with a long blink and a smile.

"Hazarding a guess," Chris paused, as he stretched out his arms and stepped back to frame the coatrack between his hands, "I would say about sixty-four inches."

"No way," Richard responded.

"Trust me, Richard," Tom added. "If Chris says it's sixty-four inches, then it is definitely sixty-four inches." Tom and Chris smiled.

Richard eyed the coatrack up and down, then looked down at Chris's shoes. "Nine-and-a-half, right?" Richard asked.

Chris looked down at his shoes then back at Richard. "Yeah."

"Pull off your right shoe," he directed, pointing with his hand, and snapping his fingers.

"What?" Chris asked.

"Your right shoe. Pull it off," Richard insisted. Chris hesitated, as he looked back down at his shoes. "Look, I wore lace-ups today and you got loafers. I need something to measure the rack height to compare with mine, and we're the same size."

"If that's all you need, I have a …," Chris stopped short. "I have to sit down." Chris sat down, pulled off his shoe, and handed it to Richard. "I typically let only professional cobblers handle my shoes, especially when they're being used as a measuring device."

"Don't worry," Richard said. "It's in good hands." He looked the shoe over, pulled a handkerchief from his pocket, and gave the shoe a light polishing.

"You're a brave man, Richard," Tom said, laughing. "That's a fungi funhouse."

"Not a problem," Richard responded. "Smelling my grandfather's shoes prepared me for almost anything." Then, after catching a whiff, "Though, this is a close second," he commented, as he knelt next to the coatrack.

"Okay," Chris said. "We can do without the colorful commentary. Just stay focused on the task at hand and overlook the distractions …and don't forget who's missing a shoe!"

Richard set the shoe heel on the floor, pointed the toe toward the top of the coatrack, and used his index finger to mark along the coatrack vertical member at the extreme end of the shoe. Once he established the location, he guided the shoe upward until the heel met his index finger and continued the process until he reached the top of the coatrack in these measured stops.

"Five and a half," Richard reported, after reaching the top.

"Five and a half what?" Tom asked.

"Five and a half nine-and-a-halves, of course," Richard responded. He flipped the shoe in his hand, grabbing the toe end midair, and handed it back to Chris. "Never hand a customer his shoe toe first," he said with a click of his tongue and a wink.

"Is that supposed to be bad luck or something?" Chris asked.

"That way, they always know the kind of heel they're looking at," Richard said. He laughed and slapped Chris's shoulder. "It's an old shoe-salesman's joke. By the way, nice shoes. Two words: baking and soda; and go a little lighter on the polish." He dangled his handkerchief for Chris to see the discolored areas from the shoe polish.

"Very funny," Chris countered, as he slipped his shoe on. "I'm already using baking soda."

"I assure you, what I smelt was not excessive shoe polish," Richard responded, as Tom laughed. "I'd increase the baking soda."

"So, how did they compare?" Tom asked. "Same height?"

"Mine is much shorter," he answered.

"You actually know how tall your coatrack, uh, stick is in shoe lengths?" Chris asked.

"I use association to help me think about things from more than one perspective," Richard responded. "It helps keep your mind sharp. For example, my desk at home is about two-and-a-half shoes tall, or about thirty inches. My computer monitor is two shoes diagonally, or about twenty-four inches. Now I know my coat stick is almost a full shoe shorter than Tom's, or about fifty-four inches tall."

"Don't all of these conversions get confusing," Chris asked. "Why don't you just use a tape measure like everyone else?"

"You have to be able to improvise in life," Richard answered. "You don't always have access to a tape measure, but you're almost always wearing shoes."

"Excellent point, Richard," Tom said, trying not to laugh. "I mean, look around the room; we're all wearing shoes."

"And I'm the lucky one wearing loafers," Chris added.

"Besides," Richard continued, "why would either of us bring a tape measure to the office? We're salesmen, not construction workers."

"I can't think of any good reason," Tom said. "You, Chris?"

"Nothing immediately comes to mind," Chris answered, as he stared back at Tom.

"Sixty-four inches," Richard said, as he eyed the coatrack and rubbed his chin. "Now that I think about it, maybe that's how I've been getting sand in the pockets of my long, dress coat."

"Sounds like you need a new coatrack," Chris said.

"No, I need a longer stick," Richard replied.

"That won't do much for the looks of things," Chris said.

"If maintenance can get my door to close, it won't matter," he added, as he walked away.

"Now that was classic," Tom said, once Richard was out of earshot.

"But not too surprising. Though I can't recall Richard ever telling so many jokes; at least, not funny ones."

"He's certainly on a roll today."

"Speaking of rolling, I need to get going. These machines aren't going to sell themselves. I'll see you later, Tom," Chris said, as he made his way toward his office.

"Smells better in here already," Tom said loud enough for Chris to hear.

"It never gets old, Tom."

"Good morning, Jack," Cheryl said, as he made his way through the front door and eased into the lobby. She watched him for a second. "You look like a scared deer in the wild trying to find out where that clicking noise is coming from."

"Oh, good morning, Cheryl," he said, loosening up a bit. "I thought I heard someone, I mean, something." Jack looked back toward the parking lot. "I didn't see Paul's car out there, so I guess he's not in."

"He was here earlier. I can get him on the phone if you need to speak with him."

"Oh, no." Jack insisted. "That's quite alright. I can catch up with him later, or whenever."

"He left right after you drove by the last time."

"Drove by?" he asked, shrugging his shoulders, and forcing a chuckle. "Who drove by?"

"That wasn't your car that drove by the shop about three times, earlier?"

"Wow! Why would I do that?" he asked, as he made his way through the lobby. "This is starting to sound like a mystery novel, Cheryl. You would make a great author," he added, as he stepped into his office. Jack dropped his shoulders, made his way over to his desk, and fell into his chair. "Loosen up," he told himself, as he swiveled his chair back and forth. "Relax for a minute, get your things together, and get out before Paul comes back.". He sat up and began pulling his folders and brochures for his morning visits. "These should keep me out the rest of the day". He placed it all in his leather satchel and scanned his desk to be sure he wasn't forgetting anything.

"Hey Paul!" Jack heard Cheryl announce, as he raised his

head in full alert.

Is he back already? He thought. He sat motionless to increase his concentration and listen for any hints of Paul's direction or intent.

"Back so soon?" Cheryl asked.

"Yeah. I forgot to take a folder with me. I'll just be a minute and then I'll be on my way …again." He made his way through the lobby and down the hall to his office.

Jack sat like a statue, staring a hole through his desk, and hoping Paul couldn't hear his heart beating. *Make like a deer in the woods, deer in the woods. Don't move. Hunter in the area. Deer in the woods.*

Paul retrieved his folder and made a quick glance into Jack's office before heading back toward the lobby. Noticing Jack at his desk, Paul stopped and leaned into the doorway. "Good morning, Jack."

Got me! "Hey, Paul. How are you?"

"Great. You sure are quiet this morning. I usually hear you doing something or talking to someone when I come in."

"Just focused on trying to get my stuff together for some customer visits, today."

"Those visits going to keep you out most of the morning?"

"Probably all day," Jack replied.

"Okay. You and I seem to keep missing each other and I'd like to have some time to talk with you. Let's get together tomorrow afternoon."

"Sure thing, Paul," Jack responded. "Anything in particular I need to prepare for?"

"Not really. I think we have all we need." Jack raised his eyebrows.

We? Jack thought. *I hope he has a mouse in his pocket.*

"I have to get going," Paul said. "I'll see you tomorrow, Jack. Have a great day."

"You, too, Paul." As Paul continued toward the lobby, Jack straightened his smile, closed his eyes, and sat still, wanting to be sure he heard Paul exit the building. Satisfied he was gone, "Who is we?" he said, "and what do WE want to talk about?" He gazed at his watch. *I'll give him a minute to get out of the parking lot,* he thought. When time had expired, he stood with his things, surveyed his office one more time, then made his way toward the lobby, giving Paul plenty of time for a good head start. "Have a great day, Cheryl," he said, as he got to the lobby. "I'll be out all day on sales calls."

"Okay, Jack. We'll see you tomorrow."

Once he made it to the parking lot, "Wait," Jack said, "We could be me and Paul! Yeah. Maybe he just wants to discuss my sales goals or update me on my numbers. I need to stay positive." He picked up his pace and began whistling, almost dancing over the small pothole in the parking lot.

Chapter 12

In less than forty-eight hours, Paul's assignment of finding another salesman was well under way. His headhunters had already culled a list of candidates from their master database and started calling the prospects Wednesday afternoon. By Thursday morning they had one possibility, a local industrial-engine salesman looking for a career change. Their next call was to Tom Brandent at Gantly Industrial Sales.

Tom should have been across town early Thursday morning, but car trouble held him up. He was thankful it happened at work, as the Gantly service shop was able to install a new battery while he waited in his office. With repairs complete and running about an hour behind schedule, he was anxious to get on his way. He had just grabbed his organizer and was about to stand and leave when his phone rang. He sat still for a moment, staring at his phone. "Why not," he grumbled. He picked up the receiver. "Good morning, this is Tom. How may I help you?"

"Good morning, Tom. This is Austin Millwright with Ballard's Associates. We are a premiere placement firm for this area and excel in matching the right person with the right job. We are currently in the market for a salesman and were wondering if you had anyone in mind who may be interested?"

Lord, please give me wisdom for this. He swiveled his chair around to view his doorway. "I may know someone, but can you tell me anything else about the company?"

"I can tell you it is a highly respected organization located in the DFW area that is positioning itself to be a major supplier of its products in all of North Central Texas. They believe in hiring only the best, which is one reason they have chosen us to search out their candidates."

"Wow, Austin. I can tell you're looking for a salesman, that all sounds pretty ambiguous. What's the product line?"

"They are a major supplier of industrial equipment, and the salesman will be responsible for marketing this and other related sundry items."

"Equipment, huh?" Tom raised an eyebrow. "I think I know someone who may be interested in discussing this further."

"Excellent. May I have their name, please?"

What if this is the call? He felt his heart start to race as his breathing became faster. He looked around his office at a few of all the mementos he had collected from his tenure at Gantly, and then glanced down at his family's photo on his desk. Tom answered, "My name is Tom Brandent." He swallowed hard. "You can use my name." Tom moved the phone from his mouth as he let out a deep exhale to calm himself. He had broken a barrier he was never brave enough to face before, and it felt relieving.

"Very good, Tom," Austin said. "I certainly appreciate your candor. Would you be available for an interview anytime soon?"

"Yes, but, if at all possible, I would like to arrange something in the evening. I don't want this to interfere with my present job situation."

"That's understandable, Tom, and very admirable," he said. "I'll get in touch with our client, relay your request, and get back in touch with you concerning an interview time. Is that alright?"

"Sure. That'll be fine."

"Can I reach you at this number again, or is there another number you prefer?"

Tom gave Austin his cell phone number to keep from arousing too much suspicion at work or concern for Linda. He would talk to her when the time was right, and only if this lead panned out. He hung up his phone, sat back in his chair, and covered his face with his hands. *No turning back now*, he thought. Maybe the call meant nothing, but he had finally allowed himself to take a chance, which would make the next opportunity easier.

Tom leaned over and prayed for a moment and was ready to go. He swiveled his chair around to stand but noticed Jonathan arriving at his office door. He sank back down. Jonathan rapped on Tom's door and announced himself. "Tom, do you have a moment?"

Tom sighed. "Sure, come on in."

Jonathan took a seat across from Tom's desk before noticing the marketing material close by. "Oh, I'm sorry, Tom. Were you about to leave? If you are, we can talk later."

"My schedule has already been shot this morning. I had car trouble earlier, so it's no bother."

"Tom," he started, as he made himself comfortable, "I just wanted to apologize for my behavior last week. I've been under a lot of stress lately to help turn this company around and I guess I let it get to me. I hope you understand."

"Sure, Jonathan," Tom said with a half-lazy eye blink, *for the umpteenth time.*

"It's just that I've been working extra diligently these past several weeks, following any credible lead that may potentially have a positive impact on our business growth."

"Yes, we've all been working extra hard, and it's not always pleasant." *Case in point*, as he made a quick smile.

"Sure, you and the rest of the sales team have been demonstrating your usual, shall we say, zealous effort, yet the needed results are much more demanding. As you can imagine, as sales manager, the weight on my shoulders from the responsibilities I carry are enormous."

"You are weighted down with a lot of things," *not to mention your ego. Lord, please forgive me, again.*

"So it's not surprising to learn these things can bring out a wide range of emotional responses, some rather intense, yet at the same time, unexpected."

"Totally unexpected," Tom added.

"And they often escalate to levels which regrettably led to our heated exchange last week, though I must admit it was a unique way to foster a teachable moment, as I'm sure you must concur."

Tom glanced back at his desk phone. "Honestly, what you said last week was very hurtful and uncalled for. I'm a man, as you are, and I deserve more respect than the brow beating you handed me. You're my supervisor and I respect you for that but would appreciate a more professional relationship."

Jonathan was taken aback by Tom's response, as he stared for a moment in disbelief. He let out a long sigh as he sat up in the chair. "I suppose you thought I had that coming," Jonathan said, leaning forward. "I guess not everyone is ready for my motivational management style," he lamented. "I admit it is a little progressive for many of your generation and it can cause a bit of friction. But, again, I want to apologize for any misunderstanding we may have had, and I will take your comments under advisement."

I don't think I got through to him. "That's great, Jonathan," he said with a tang of sarcasm. "I appreciate you coming in here and approaching me about this."

"I just thought it best that we quickly settle these things in the open and not let them fester."

They both sat there for a moment. Tom was nodding his head with tight lips. "It sounds like we have something to build on." Then, looking at his watch, Tom said, "Oh my! I need to get going."

"Oh, by all means." They both stood as Tom prepared to leave.

"Have a good day, Jonathan." Tom grabbed his things and headed out, leaving Jonathan standing at his desk.

"You, too, my boy," Jonathan watched Tom walk out. "Oh these young kids," Jonathan said. "They are so predictable and impressionable. I believe he's coming around." Jonathan stood there for a moment, smiling, before straightening his tie and heading back to his office.

Tom allowed himself plenty of drive time for the local highways, especially for scheduled business appointments across town, but today's late start was almost too much. He wasn't in the lobby long before his new, potential customer came to get him.

"Tom?"

"Yes."

"Kenny Woods," the loud voice said.

"Thanks for seeing me, Kenny." Kenny looked around the area where Tom had been sitting. Thinking he had dropped something, Tom gave the lobby a good scan.

"You got everything? No loose bags or anything?"

"Just what I have in my hands."

"Okay."

"Sorry I'm late. It's just been one of those days."

"It happens. Come on back." Kenny escorted Tom into his office and offered him a comfortable, leather chair. "I have only a few minutes before my next appointment."

Tom looked around at the nice furnishings and noted the efficient size and layout of the office. A place for everything, and everything in its place. "You guys have a very nice facility."

"We're new in town. Just opened the doors a couple of months ago and still in the process of moving from Illinois to take advantage of the warmer weather down here. It won't take long for this place to look lived-in, especially once our crews start getting busy." Kenny looked over at the items Tom was holding. "Are you sure you got everything, didn't leave anything in the lobby or in the car?"

"Oh no, I have everything with me." Tom reached to extend Kenny his business card. "I wanted to come by and formally introduce myself. As I said on the phone, Gantly offers a wide variety of industrial equipment to fit most needs. I remember you said Davidson Drilling was trying to branch off into some new areas, possibly requiring some new equipment. I assume that's related to the move?"

"It's our opinion this area offers many opportunities for growth. We currently have four field crews and hope to be adding one or two more over time and will need equipment to support them. Nothing immediate, you understand, but eventually." He took a quick glance at his watch.

"I brought along these brochures for you to look over. The sizes and models would match your needs, based on what you were able to tell me yesterday."

Kenny took the brochures, glanced at their photos, and tossed them to one side of his desk. "I'll keep these on file for when the time comes." A little surprised, Tom sat bewildered, as Kenny's phone rang. "Let me get this. It's probably our receptionist."

"Sure," Tom said. *It's not like we're discussing business anyway.*

"This is Kenny. Oh, hi, Olivia. Jack is here? Great! I'll come get him in a minute."

"I guess your next appointment is here."

"Yes, but he went to the restroom. If you've got anything else to show me, we can take a couple minutes."

"Oh no, I'm done," Tom said, as he gathered his things and stood. "Sometimes I get carried away and don't know when to stop. I appreciate you giving me the time to come by to see you. I can see my way out."

"Thanks, Tom. Come by anytime." Tom walked to the lobby and approached the receptionist desk to sign out in the register. He scanned the list of visitor entries and there it was, right below his:

Jack Fisher. I've heard a lot about him but have never met him. I wonder—

"Jack," Kenny called out. "Good to see you again." Tom turned his head toward the hallway but caught only a glimpse of the back side of a sports coat as Jack turned the corner. "What's in the bag?" he heard Kenny ask. He heard a muffled response from Jack, followed by, "For me?"

"Sounds like someone found their lost bag," Tom murmured.

"Did you say something, sir?" Olivia asked.

"Oh no. I mean, yes, I did, but no. I just thought of something, that's all. Have a good day." On the way to his car, he tried to debrief himself. "That was an awkward kind of a meeting." Once inside, he sat still for a moment, rehearsing the scene again. "You know it's bad when it gets hard to tell the difference between reality and the movie playing in your head." With time to kill, he decided to call Daniel. "Good morning, Daniel, it's Tom. I was wondering how the conversation went with your dad."

"Mm, I haven't talked with him yet, Tom," he said. "We've all been really busy and everything."

Tom closed his eyes and shook his head; thankful Daniel couldn't see his response. "I know it's none of my business, but if it wasn't so awkward, I'd talk with Albert myself. I realize he doesn't owe me an explanation about his money affairs, and I'm not trying to be nosey, but I'm concerned for you and your dad, and your business. The last thing I want is to appear to your dad as just another whiney salesman who lost a contract and feels he's owed a satisfactory explanation from the customer."

"I appreciate that, Tom, and so would Dad. I'll try to talk to him this afternoon, after everyone else leaves. That way, if he blows up, it'll just be him and me."

"Let me know how it goes."

"Sure, Tom. I'll call you tomorrow."

After hanging up the phone, Tom took a moment to pray that Daniel would have the courage to talk with his dad.

Thursday afternoon, Paul and Jack walked into Bill's office, and Paul closed the door behind them. Bill was seated behind his desk with his reading glasses on, rearranging the folders in front of him that he had put together for the meeting. "Come on in, guys, and have a seat," Bill said, pointing to the seats in front of his desk, as he removed his reading glasses and laid them on his desk.

Jack's busy schedule was interrupted with a surprise invitation to attend this gathering and was clueless as to what it was about, but the somber tone told him it wasn't good. Courteous smiles all around, no uninvited conversation, no unintentional noise …just quiet. Every sound seemed amplified: the squeak of the chairs, the whirl of the air from the air-conditioning duct, his heartbeat, the tapping of his shoes…. *My shoes are tapping! Stop!*

"Jack," Bill began, "I've asked you to come in here to help clear up, what appear to be, some disturbing matters regarding questionable conduct over the last year or so; specifically, your conduct." Jack raised his eyebrows. "I've asked Paul to be here because he's your direct supervisor. It's not that I don't think Paul could have handled this himself, but I wanted you to know how serious I consider these issues to be."

Jack was already uncomfortable from the gloomy atmosphere, and now they wanted to discuss his questionable conduct. He tried to hold back the surprised, guilty look on his face. He began to retrace every encounter he could think of that might have been considered shady, trying to determine if he had left any loose ends. *Who could have messed this deal up? It's so simple. Gary! That's what got him fired!* His nervousness was obvious, as he interlocked his hands in his lap and began tapping his thumbs together. "Sure, Mr. Redding," Jack responded. "I'll do what I can to help clear this up." *Stop the thumb tapping! Calm down!*

"Good." Bill opened his first folder with the contracts he and

134

Paul had reviewed on Tuesday and laid it flat on his desk. "Now, Jack, I'm not going to start throwing allegations at you, or screaming and ranting. But I will tell you that these folders contain evidence of some very suspicious and blatantly unethical activities. Instead, I'd rather give you the opportunity to come clean with Paul and me about how you have been conducting your business over the last year or so."

Jack tried to stall for time, shaking his head and biting his lower lip. *Think, think, think. What are they after? How much do they know?* "Mr. Redding, I'm not sure how to address this."

"Let me get you started," Bill offered, as he put on his reading glasses and looked over the contracts in front of him. "Are you familiar with a company called Beckett Construction?" Bill glanced over at Jack while peering over his reading glasses.

"I sold them a small machine about five months ago. I didn't accidentally write that up as a taxable sale, did I?" he asked, trying to be coy. Bill responded with a brief, hard stare. "I'll take that as a no," Jack responded.

"Do you remember any special contractual obligations beyond our normal terms and conditions?"

Contractual obligations? Is there some new IRS rule I'm not following? Just stick to your guns; but be serious. "Not that I can recall," Jack answered. "That was a pretty standard contract,"—*for me.*

Bill handed the office copy of the original contract to Jack. "Is this the contract you signed with Beckett Construction?"

Take your time. Pretend you're reading it carefully. You need time to think. Jack glanced down at the bottom of the contract. *Whew, he thought. No special instructions. This is the office copy of the contract. If this is all they have, they've got nothing!* "Yes, this looks like the contract we signed," Jack answered. "Is there a problem with it?"

"Not by itself. But compare it to this contract." Bill handed Jack the copy Steven had obtained from Mr. Beckett.

Jack recognized the document immediately, though he tried not to show it. He swallowed hard as he took a deep, long look. *Of all the people I could have teamed up with, I had to pick Alan.* "Where did this copy come from?" Jack's right leg began bouncing, and he laid his right hand on his thigh to steady it.

"Last week, Mr. Alan Beckett brought this machine in for some service work. After learning the only problem was with the filters, he produced this document, which shows Landover is responsible for all the maintenance for the first six months. We were obligated by this contract to do the work for free."

Jack sat spellbound, unsure of what to do next. He had never been any good at chess, but he knew enough to recognize his king was in trouble. *If the contracts are all they have I can get out of this. I'll just move my bishop to cover my king.* Jack closed his eyes as he whispered his confession, "He was supposed to call me."

Bill leaned forward a little more to hear Jack. "What was that, Jack?"

Jack opened his eyes. "Alan. Alan was supposed to call me. I told him if he ever had trouble to call me first."

"What do you mean, call you first?" Bill asked.

"He was supposed to call me before he called the service department or anyone else. If he doesn't call me first, too many people get involved and information gets leaked, and that ruins everything."

"But I don't understand, Jack. Why the secrecy? I mean, we've given away things like this before to customers as part of the deal. Why did you feel the need to write a separate contract and hide it?"

Jack swallowed hard, embarrassed to reveal his greed. "When free maintenance is part of a standard contract, it goes against the gross profit of the job, lowering my commission. If I can work around the system and keep the customer happy, I make more money."

"But, Jack, where are you writing off the expenses?"

"I know this is going to sound like just another stupid, selfish stunt pulled off by a greedy salesman, but this is how it works." *Throw in some appearance of old-fashioned repentance and all will be forgiven.* "The customer is supposed to call me first when their filters need changing. Most customers are willing to do routine maintenance themselves, especially if I bring them free consumables, which I do to limit the number of service calls. I assign the filters to our Customer Relations account or our Company Policy account. If a service call has to be made, I get the respective purchasing agent to pay for it with their credit card, and then I turn it in as an expense, like extra mileage, to pay them back."

Bill and Paul both sat silent for a moment, staring at Jack in disbelief with their chins dropped and their mouths open, unable to move a muscle. Jack had rattled off his process so efficiently, it sounded as though he was reading an actual policy from the company handbook.

"Whew," Jack said, as he released a big sigh, looking relieved. "I feel so much better now, having gotten that off my chest."

Bill pulled himself together, blinking his eyes several times. "Jack, what you have just described to us is a multiplicity of improprieties, some even possibly prosecutable by law. And this is just the contracts!"

Just the contracts? What else do they know? Now he felt his king surrounded, as he imagined Bill's knight taking his bishop. The only thing that came to mind was, *Checkmate! Game over!*

"I can't fully express to you the hurt and disappointment Paul and I feel, concerning what we have learned in the last few months about your dealings: the double set of contracts, the untimely, personal gifts. These are unacceptable means of procuring sales for Landover; and I'm sure Paul had gone over such inappropriate tactics with you at some point during your early training." Paul acknowledged by nodding his head. Jack just sat there.

So much for a fool-proof plan, Jack thought.

"These acts, Jack, are selfish and greedy, and demonstrate, to a degree, your lack of character. I will admit, to the best we can estimate, they have not been a large financial burden to the company yet, maybe between ten and twenty-thousand dollars, but that's not the point. In fact, we may have been willing to spend this money to get the kind of contracts that were brought in, but we would have done it in an ethical and transparent manner. You have taken advantage of the company, its employees, and our customer base, and profited on every side. Yes, you've brought in a lot of sales over the last two years, but now I must ask myself whether you were able to do this because you're a great salesman or a great showman."

Jack lowered his eyes to the top of Bill's desk. "You're right, Mr. Redding," Jack acknowledged, "about everything." He raised his eyes to look at Bill. "But it's not all my fault," he pleaded. Bill and Paul raised their eyebrows and pulled their heads back. "I mean, if the system allowed it to happen, then why is it all my fault? Maybe there should be some safety nets to watch for this type of activity before it gets this far. Maybe I'm just a victim consumed by the over-demanding business world—"

"Jack," Bill interrupted, "I'm going to give you the best advice I could ever give anyone, and that is, never lie to yourself." Jack sat perplexed. "You see, Jack, you can lie to me, you can lie to Paul, and you can even lie to God, though He knows the truth, but never lie to yourself. Because when you start lying to yourself, you start believing everything you say, and you convince yourself you're always right and never in need of repentance. If you never lie to yourself, even though you do lie to those around you, at least your conscience will continue to remind you of your faults, and repentance will not be far away." Bill paused before delivering his verdict. "With that being said, it's my decision to let you go today."

Jack sunk in his seat. "Is there anything I can do to make you change your mind, Mr. Redding?"

"I'm afraid not, Jack, I've made up my mind. Based on the gravity of these actions, I must abide by my decision."

Jack sat silent for a moment. "Very well, Mr. Redding. I appreciate the opportunity I have been given here at Landover."

Then turning toward Paul, "Thank you, Paul, for your help and leadership, and I apologize for not living up to your expectations."

"Thank you for your hard work," Paul responded. "I hope you apply these lessons learned in your next endeavor."

"I guess I'll clear out what I can today. Do you mind if I come back on Monday morning to get what I leave behind? I was taking off tomorrow anyway because my wife is having another prenatal checkup, and then we're going out of town."

"Sure," Bill responded. "Monday will be fine. But I'll have to ask you for your cell phone, company ID and credit card now."

Jack reached for his wallet and pulled out his company credit card, and removed his ID badge and phone, and laid it all on Bill's desk. "I've also got an office key, too," he said as he removed it from his keychain and handed it to Bill.

"Again, Jack, I'm sorry it came to this, but I think you understand."

"Sure, sure, I understand. I guess I'll start clearing out."

They all stood to their feet. Jack shook hands with each of them and walked out of Bill's office, leaving the door open.

"I think he has some real talent," Paul said, as he and Bill stared at the empty doorway.

"Yes. But talent is like a lion. With character, it doesn't have to prove anything and takes only its share. Without character, it must always be the victor and is never satisfied with what it has."

Jack walked down the hallway to his office, trying to keep his head up. It wouldn't take long for the news to spread through the entire company. *How humiliating!* He went to his desk, fell into his chair, and stared at the wall for a moment trying to take it all in. He swiveled his chair in a complete circle, taking mental photographs of everything in the room and rehearsing all the great memories of working at Landover. He came to a stop in front of his desk, as he leaned over and dropped his face in his hands. "What am I going to tell Paula?" he whispered.

As he contemplated his next move, he thought of his lunch

last Friday with Jonathan. He had given Jack plenty of time to make up his mind. Surely, Jonathan wouldn't mind an early phone call. To ensure his privacy, Jack got up from his chair and walked to his office door. He stuck his head out into the hallway and looked to his left to be sure no one was coming. Then he looked to his right and saw Jerry coming down the hallway.

"Hey, Jack," Jerry called out.

Jack dropped his head and closed his eyes. "Hey, Jerry," Jack responded in a subdued tone.

"I just wanted you to know that I didn't forget about you."

"What do you mean?"

"Your wrist rest." Jerry produced a wrist rest and showed it to Jack. "Gel-filled, antimicrobial, and the latest in ergonomic design."

"Oh, yeah, the wrist rest," he responded. Jerry walked on into Jack's office, as Jack tried to dissuade him. "You don't have to do that now, do you, Jerry?"

Jerry continued his march to Jack's desk, as Jack followed him over. "Oh, this will only take a second." Jerry grabbed the old wrist rest. "Out with the old," he said, placing it in the trash can under Jack's desk, "and in with the new." He positioned the pad in front of the keyboard. "Try it," he said, as he stood back and gestured with his hands.

Jack just stood there, not sure what to do. *The last thing I need right now is a wrist rest.*

"Go ahead, Jack, don't be shy. It won't hurt you." Jack sat down at his desk and, using the wrist rest, pretended to type on the keyboard, as Jerry pushed his glasses further up on his nose and leaned over Jack's shoulder. "Now doesn't that feel better?"

"Uh, yeah, it sure does," Jack answered, feeling a little awkward and foolish. "Thanks, for bringing it by."

"I'm glad I could help," he replied. "I guess I better get going. I've got to deliver another whoopee cushion to Margaret. She wears those things out faster than I do headbands for my safety goggles," Jerry said chuckling. "See you around."

Jerry walked out and Jack followed him to the doorway. Again, he looked left and right down the hallway and saw no one, so he closed his door and locked it to eliminate any further interruptions. He walked back to his desk and sat down, found Jonathan's number, and placed his call.

"Good afternoon, Gantly Industrial Sales," Claire, answered.

"Jonathan Edwards, please." Jack's heart was beginning to race as he waited for Jonathan to pick up the line, not sure how to start the conversation. "Don't sound desperate", he repeated to himself.

"Sales, Jonathan Edwards speaking."

"Mr. Edwards," he said. "This is Jack Fisher. You and I had lunch last week at McCardy's."

"Yes, of course, Jack," Jonathan answered. "What can I do for you, my boy?"

"Mr. Edwards, during lunch, you and I discussed some possible opportunities about my future." Jack paused to give Jonathan a chance to confirm his offer but was met with immediate silence. *Hello, Jonathan. Don't leave me hanging. Anytime now. Please don't tell me you changed your mind.*

"Yes, Jack," Jonathan answered. "We discussed matters of great importance to both of us. Of which matter do I owe the pleasure of this conversation?"

"I was wondering if your job offer was still open," he said.

"Certainly, Jack!" Jack let out a quiet sigh of relief. "As we discussed, I didn't need an immediate answer, so I've simply been allowing you the time you need to make your decision."

"I've made my decision, or to be honest with you, the decision was made for me. You see, Mr. Edwards," Jack admitted, "I just got fired. My employer didn't like the way I made a few sales, so, now I need a job."

"Rest assured, Jack, you have a job here", Jonathan replied without hesitation. "Your present employer simply has not recognized your ability to flourish where others may flounder. Don't worry about a thing. You can start your new job immediately."

"May I come in on Monday morning?"

"You can come in tomorrow, if you like, Jack."

"My wife and I are expecting our first baby in a few months, and she has a doctor's appointment tomorrow, all the way across town, and she wants me to be there. So, Monday would be a better fit."

"Congratulations, my boy. Monday is not a problem. In fact," Jonathan hesitated, as he pieced together a plan, "be here promptly at 9:00am. It's a little later than our normal start time, but it will give me an opportunity to pull everyone together and preface them before your grand introduction. May we call this your official acceptance of my offer?"

"Yes, certainly, Mr. Edwards; and thank you for believing in me. I hope you can use my talent."

"Jack, consider today, your day of release. Talent is like a lion. When subdued, it will only take what it is given. When released to its natural bidding, it will devour and reign supreme. You, Jack, have talent, and starting Monday I'll show you how to use it."

"Thank you, Mr. Edwards. I'll see you Monday morning at 9:00am sharp." Jack hung up the phone and sunk in his chair, cupped his hands over his face, and tried to relax his body. "That's a relief," he said, "though it felt a little creepy. Now, what do I tell Paula?" Jack sat for a few minutes to let his mind catch up with reality, as everything seemed to be registering. He just got fired from a job he loved, he just got hired by a man he barely knew, his wife doesn't know yet, and he has no character. *No character?* he thought. *Who does Bill think he is to tell me that?* The guilt began to mount, and he knew if Paul were in the room, he'd confess everything. After a few quiet moments of self-reflection, his defense mechanism kicked in, the guilt subsided, and Jack was ready to move on. *Maybe it'll all be different once I start the new job. Hopefully, Monday will change everything.*

As Jack finally awoke to the realization he no longer worked at Landover, he surveyed his office and devised a plan to remove his personal effects in a manner to draw as little attention from his coworkers as possible. He loaded what he could in a large box and left several books and other small items for Monday morning. One box of items out the door wouldn't appear suspicious to anyone, but, tomorrow, everyone would know.

He opened his office door to assess his exit strategy and sensed a green light. He slipped out into the hallway and closed the door behind him to keep his disheveled office from being discovered before Monday, or at least until he made it to the parking lot. Once he reached the lobby, he made a beeline to the front door, but the bulky load he carried required that he turn around to let himself out.

"Are you gone for the day?" Cheryl asked.

"Yes, I am, Cheryl," he answered, as he glanced toward the receptionist's desk, never making eye contact. "Good evening."

Chapter 13

Ray left work a little early Thursday evening to check out Bruno's, recommended by Cliff and just a couple of miles from the shop. He was hoping it would be similar to the last place he frequented, just a plain, traditional, men's barber shop—nothing with the words Salon or Boutique in the title—where he could get a simple haircut, not the latest style. As he approached the building front, he noticed the familiar candy-striped pole outside, which he considered a good omen, and the sign above the door, Bruno's Cuts, more good news. He walked inside and noticed the atmosphere was laid back and comfortable by most male standards: sports memorabilia on the walls, an assortment of sports and business magazines thrown about, nice, leather chairs in the waiting area, and a large television where everyone could see, but no remote in sight; Bruno controlled the multi-media, and today, it was all stock-market news, all day.

"Welcome to Bruno's," a rough voice called from one of the cutting stations at the back of the room. Ray's attention was automatically drawn to the stout-framed, bearded man, with scissors in his hand. "Just sign in, and we'll be right with you. There are about three guys ahead of you."

"Thanks," Ray answered, as he made his way to the clear,

glass counter, which also served as a display case. He signed his name on the register as he gazed at the autographed sports gear behind the glass panes then sauntered over to one of the chairs lining the perimeter of the room. He glided himself over the seat cushion, noting the soft leather. "Wow, this is great!" he whispered. He continued his survey of the room, admiring the various artifacts hung on the walls, and recognized photos of several notable sports figures, each signed with a special thank you to Bruno. Turning toward the television, he tried to listen to the stock reports but, since he wasn't an avid investor or market watcher, it grew boring. Settling in, he looked around for some reading material and grabbed one of the business magazines lying close by that seemed to cater to the construction trade, The Earth Movers and Shakers. He glanced over the magazine cover and in the background of one of the cover-page photos was a small image of a Gantly tractor, which caught his attention. Curious, he opened the magazine to see if there were any related articles.

"Are you in the construction business?" a fellow patron asked.

Ray turned to see the balding, grey-haired man sitting next to him. "Yes sir, I am," he answered, then returned to the magazine and continued his search.

After a short silence, "What do you do?" the man followed up.

Again, Ray turned to face the man—a little slower this time—to address his question. "I'm the service manager for a local equipment distributor, Gantly Industrial Sales."

Before Ray could return to his quest, "Then you must know Cliff Tolliver the parts manager," the man added.

Surprised, Ray's eyes opened wide. "You know Cliff?"

The man used his hands as he described Cliff's typical cut. "Over the ears, a little tight on the sides, long enough on top to comb it back like he's from the fifties, but no oil. He parts it on the left …"

"to hide the scar on the right," they both said together, finishing with a smile.

"I know all of Bruno's customers," the man continued. "I come here almost every day to have something to do; unless, of course, my wife gets me started on one of her projects before I manage to get out the door," he chuckled, "and I love to talk to people. Besides, Bruno's a pretty good guy," he said, looking back at the cutting stations, loud enough for Bruno to hear.

"You got that right, Harold," Bruno responded.

The man turned back to Ray. "By the way, I guess you know now, my name is Harold."

"It's good to meet you, Harold. My name is Ray."

"As you can also tell, it doesn't take long for me to get a haircut with what little hair I have left." He pointed at the narrow, semicircular region on the back of his head. "Having such a limited amount of hair also has its advantages. I only get charged for a beard trim. But the bad part is," he said with a more serious, thoughtful look, "Bruno makes me sit in the chair backward when he cuts it." They both started laughing.

"That's pretty funny," Ray responded.

"Don't encourage him," Bruno interjected. "That's the third time this week he's used that joke."

Ray was enjoying the conversation and glad Harold was there to break up the monotony. He figured Bruno didn't mind either, since Harold's conversation seemed to help make the time go by quicker for everyone in the waiting area.

"Have you found anything interesting in that magazine to read?" Harold pointed at the cover.

"I thought there might be an article on this Gantly tractor shown in the background of this photo," he said, pointing at the cover page.

Harold leaned his head back a little to see the photo through his bifocals. "That's a Billston tractor with a few after-market modifications," he said. "I'm surprised neither Cliff nor I saw that last week when he was reading that same magazine."

Ray gave a closer look, scanning the photo until he saw the Billston logo, almost hidden behind one of those after-market add-ons Harold referred to. "You're right, Harold, and Gantly is a Billston distributor. You must be in the construction business yourself, to be that familiar with this type of heavy machinery."

"Thirty years at the Billston Minnesota plant," he proclaimed. "My wife and I moved down here five years ago, right after I retired. Speaking of the wife," he said, glancing at the clock on the wall, "I need to get going. I told her I would be home twenty minutes ago. It was nice to meet you, Ray."

Harold walked out the door, as Ray went back to his magazine. He skimmed over the table of contents and found an article of interest; Increasing Your Profits: Going Green to Stay in the Black. He flipped to the story and scanned it over, catching a word phrase here and there, which began to ring familiar: increase profits, environmental fees, apply to all purchases, few complaints. Sensing an instance of déjà vu, Ray decided to read the entire article. "Cliff," he muttered to himself, about halfway through, "so this is where you do your industrial analysis and find your cutting-edge ideas. I had to actually work on my idea, and you get yours from a barbershop magazine. You lazy, little—"

"Ray!" a voice called from the cutting stations. Ray's heart jumped, as he looked up. "You're next."

Late nights were normal for Daniel, as the quiet evenings offered him the uninterrupted time he needed to organize his workflow and maintenance schedules. Tonight, he focused on completing a spare parts list he needed to order the next day. Being single, the long hours didn't bother him; after all, someday this business would be his, and he still had a lot to learn.

It was after seven o'clock when he called it quits, but on his way out he noticed his father's office light was still on. He walked down the hall and saw his father sitting in his chair with his back to the doorway, facing the credenza behind his desk and staring at his monitor. Albert appeared to be in deep thought, almost staring right through the flickering screen saver. At first, Daniel thought he would just say goodnight to his father and leave but then remembered the promise he had made to Tom. He stood at the doorway for a few moments trying to work up the inner courage to speak and then rapped on the door. Albert jumped then spun his chair around to see who it was.

"Hey, Son. Are you about to leave?" Albert rolled his chair up to his desk and closed the partly open, top-right desk drawer.

"Yeah, Dad, I was just fixing to take off and I noticed your light was still on."

"I'll lockup if you want to go ahead and get home. I was about to go myself."

"I'll wait on you." Daniel's mind raced to scramble together something to say, as he watched Albert straighten some paperwork on his desk, scribble a few notes, and put away some files into his desk drawers.

"That's about that." Albert gave his desktop one last visual inspection. "I guess we can leave now." As Albert started to stand, Daniel spoke.

"Dad, if you've got a few minutes, I'd like to talk to you about something," he said.

"Sure, Son, come on in and have a seat," Albert replied, as he took his seat again. Daniel walked in and sat across from Albert.

"Dad, I don't know how to begin other than to say that I'm a little concerned about our business. I know you take care of all the main finances, but someday I'm going to have to learn how to handle it myself."

"I know, Son, and it will all come in time, but why the sudden interest?"

"We just made a very large purchase from Landover, the largest single purchase I believe we've ever made, certainly that I can remember. I know this kind of equipment cost a lot of money, much more than what we are spending on keeping the old equipment going."

"That's true, but for a company to keep moving, much less grow, it's got to spend money. You know what kind of shape our older equipment is in. Some of it is an embarrassment to send to a customer's job site. You've done a remarkable job keeping the old stuff operating but we needed this new equipment. When you start retiring some of the older machines in a couple of years, you'll be glad we bought it."

"But that's just it, Dad. Our new equipment cost a lot of money."

"That's true, Son, but so did your braces." They both smiled.

"Seriously, Dad, you know I quote most all our work, and I buy pretty much all our parts and supplies. I hire contractors to fix things here at the office, and I pay the bills to get our service trucks repaired. In other words, I don't have the whole picture, but I've got a pretty good idea of how much money is coming in and going out of our business."

"So, tell me, Daniel, just how are we doing?"

"I would say that we were doing excellent before the new purchase," Daniel said.

"And with the new purchase?"

"Based on what I know and the numbers I've seen, I don't understand how we can make it."

"I must say, I'm pleasantly surprised by your analytical reasoning, Daniel, but, as you said, you don't have the whole picture. Someday you'll understand that things are not always as bleak as they appear. Sometimes you must go through a rough spot, but it usually always works out. Let me assure you that I am doing my best to keep the company in good standing." He paused as Daniel sat silent. "Does that help alleviate your concern?"

Daniel searched for words as he thought about how simple Albert made it all sound, but he knew there had to be more to it. "Maybe you haven't noticed, but I've seen you change over the last few months. You approach things differently; you stay later at work, and I wonder how much of it is because of the new purchase."

"Of course, things are different, Son. That's why it's called business. I have to change because the business demands it. There's more planning involved, more financial decisions to consider, and it all takes extra time. It will soon settle down to a reasonable level and things will change again for the better."

"What about raises, Dad? Last year you froze all increases to get us through a rough period, and now we have this major purchase to overcome. Business seems to be getting better, but will the company be able to afford wage increases this year?"

"There are many variables involved in making a decision regarding raises," Albert responded. "This new purchase is just one of them. Granted, it is the largest variable, but I am looking at everything very hard. I realize no one got a raise last year, and the last thing I want to do is postpone them again this year, but I've also got to be realistic, even to the point of accepting the possibility that there won't be any raises this year." Albert lowered his head and rubbed his palms together. "It's not what I want, Son," Albert admitted, as he looked up at Daniel. "I hope you can understand that, and believe me when I tell you, it's not what I want." Daniel could see the pain in his father's face, though Albert did his best to try to hide it.

"It sounds like the machinery purchase has put us in a real bind."

"But we needed the machinery."

"All of it?" he questioned. "I mean, we had an offer from Gantly for four pieces, and then, without warning, we're getting five from Landover. And the fifth piece is a very large machine. Do we really need all five?"

"We have made a deal for five pieces, and we will pay for five pieces!" Albert belted.

"But, Dad, if this machinery is going to drag the company down, I feel we need to consider some drastic measures."

"Like what?" Albert asked, raising his voice. "Would you propose we not have any new equipment, to continue with the old machines until they literally fall apart?"

"That's not what I would propose at all," Daniel responded in a calm voice. "But what if we sold the larger machine? Wouldn't that reduce our debt to a more manageable size?"

"No!" Albert said, as he pounded his desk. "We will not change anything!" He pushed himself up from his chair and walked over to a window, where he opened the blind and looked out at the streetlights and nearby traffic. "We will not change anything," Albert said after a short silence, in a more subdued voice. "A Torres does not go back on his word. A Torres does not run from a fight. A Torres finishes what he starts." Albert hesitated. "I hope you understand what I am saying, Son," he said, staring out the window. Daniel was at a loss for words, almost feeling ashamed for putting his father through this agony, yet he felt better it was all out in the open. Albert closed the window blind and then turned to face Daniel, while standing behind his chair, with his hands clutching the top of the chair back. "I'm sorry, Son, but I guess Jack Fisher is a better salesman than I am a businessman."

"Don't say that, Dad." Albert hung his head. "So, what are we going to do?"

"Let me worry about that, Daniel," Albert answered. "I'm working on a plan I will implement in the very near future that I believe will provide more than enough funds to get the company out of debt, much quicker than the loan from the bank requires, but you'll have to be strong. Can you do that for me, Son?"

"Sure, Dad, whatever it takes."

Albert walked over to where Daniel was sitting and placed his hand on his shoulder. "Don't worry, Daniel, I am confident you have what it takes to get through this. You'll do alright."

"I know we will, Dad."

"Good. Let's go home. I'm surprised your mother hasn't called me yet," he said, looking at his watch. Daniel stood and

Albert embraced him, slapping him gently on the back and grabbing the back of his head. It had been a long time since Albert had shown this much affection toward Daniel. Perhaps this evening had cleared up a lot of things.

Chapter 14

Friday morning started off busy for Tom. He was already on his way to his first appointment of the morning when his personal cell phone rang. "This is Tom," he answered.

"Good morning, Tom, this is Austin Millwright with Ballard's Associates. I'm calling regarding the conversation we had the other day about an open sales position with one of our clients. I just wanted you to know that our client was very impressed with your credentials and would like to arrange a meeting with you."

"Sure, Austin. Just let me know when and where."

"I know you had requested an evening interview, but they would like to meet you today for lunch. Is this too soon?"

"Sure, lunch today would be fine."

"Great. How about a place called McCardy's?"

"I know where that is. It's a great place. What time do I need to be there and how will I know who I'm meeting?"

"Be there at noon and ask for Paul Grissom at the host station."

"I'll do that. Thanks, Austin."

Tom hung up his phone and melted into his chair, realizing everything was coming together so easy—perhaps, too easy. He began to pray that God would work things out according to His perfect will.

At 9:30am sharp, Charles arrived at the office. It had been a week since his staff had implemented their new programs, and he was hoping for at least some rough indicators as to how they were doing. Everyone else was in the boardroom when he came in, and he closed the door behind him. Noticing Charles's tie was spot on, Ray turned to Darryl.

"Draw," he whispered. Darryl gave a discreet thumbs-up and a short nod.

"Good morning, everyone," Charles said, as he set down his coffee cup and notepad.

"Good morning, Mr. Gantly," the group replied. Jonathan sat sideways at the opposite end of the table, unresponsive to the greeting, preoccupied with a cuticle inspection.

Charles had forgotten to stop by his office and leave his suit jacket and hat, so he took them off in the boardroom and laid them in an empty chair before sitting down. Feeling somewhat obligated to join the group, Jonathan sighed as he swiveled his chair to face the table.

"I guess we all know why we're here."

Not all of us, Jonathan thought, as he used his silk tie to wipe across the crystal lens of his diamond-studded timepiece. *There are more important things I could be doing.*

"Last week we discussed a couple of new ideas and have since implemented them into our daily routine. I'd like to take some time this morning to discuss where we are with these ideas and see if we can determine whether they're making any noticeable impact in our business, good or bad."

Charles took his reading glasses from his shirt pocket and put them on, and then positioned his notepad to record anything of interest. Bored, Jonathan covered his mouth with his hands to hide his yawn, though his tightly closed eyes gave it away; thankfully, no one was watching him.

"Ray, let's start with your idea of offering free service based on accumulated points. First, I want you to explain how the offer is supposed to work, and then tell us how it's doing."

"Last week we started a promotional that awards customers a specific number of points for each of the different types of service work they have performed through our shop. For example, a tune-up is worth twenty-five points, an engine overhaul one-hundred-fifty points, and so on. These point totals continue to accumulate over a calendar year for each respective customer. As a customer's point total increases, it eventually reaches a level that will allow him to redeem a certain number of these points for free service. For example, five-hundred points can be redeemed for a free tune-up.

"We immediately began calling some of our larger customers who have multiple pieces of equipment to alert them of our new program. So far, it has been very receptive. After all, it's not costing the customer anything, and they will eventually get some type of free service. It has drawn in additional service work from the competition, and some of our steady customers have scheduled to bring in equipment for service that they typically would have waited on, just to increase their point total for the year. It's only been a week, but it looks very promising."

"Jeffery, what does the P&L reflect, regarding this new program?"

"To date, Mr. Gantly, we have not been out any cost, with exception to the printing cost for the flyers. I spoke with Ray about this program yesterday and one of those steady customers he referred to has a relatively large equipment fleet. They have already directed enough business to our shop to come close to qualifying for a free service. I think if we give it a few more weeks we'll have a better understanding of how profitable it's going to be, but, all in all, it looks like we are going to come out on top with this idea."

Pennies and nickels, Jonathan thought. *We could collect aluminum cans to generate the same amount of net revenue.* He smiled at his own joke, which gave the others the false impression he applauded Ray's idea.

"Great job, Ray," Darrell said.

"Yes, that was a good report," Charles added, as he made his notes. "Let's keep getting the word out and see what we can generate. Cliff, go ahead and explain your environmental fees plan, and give us an idea how it's going."

"Sure, Mr. Gantly. Last week we began charging our customers an environmental fee for all parts sales. There are parts that carry a specific environmental fee that we have always charged for, and these fees are tacked on top of the new fee. The total fee we now charge is a percentage of the gross sale, regardless of the items purchased.

"In regard to how it's going, I'm afraid it has not been very successful! We have had a steady line of customers show up at the cashier window and complain about the new fee. They understood what the old specific-item fees were for, but they cannot understand the new fee. I spend almost half my day explaining the new fee to customers, but they don't want it explained, they want it removed from their bill. Though it's only been a week, I have noticed that some of our major parts customers have reduced their regular purchases, opting to shop for a better price."

"Also, Mr. Gantly," Jeffrey added, "it is showing up on the P&L in reduced parts-counter sales. The environmental fee account is accruing at a faster rate than before, but it's not hard to see that the minor increase is far outweighed by the loss of revenue from reduced parts sales. At present, it doesn't look like the project is working."

Charles sat for a moment, rubbing his chin, deep in thought. "I'm torn between letting this go on for another week or two, to see if it levels out or trends the other way, and just pulling the plug on it early. From what I've heard, it doesn't look promising." He paused for a moment. "It sounds like we need to abandon this idea before we burn any more bridges and lose additional customers. Cliff, I want you to print some flyers to let our customers know we are listening to them. Tell them we have heard their complaints and have decided to abolish the new environmental fees—something like that. You know what we need to say."

"Sure, Mr. Gantly, we'll get right on it."

"Now last week, Cliff, you said you were working on some other ideas. Anything you can present today?"

Cliff looked a little surprised by the question, as he stared at Charles. "Other ideas? Of course, my other ideas. Those ideas involve …establishing things …that change our methods …yet maintain systems …" Everyone began leaning toward Cliff as if they were trying to help pull the words out of his mouth. Then, finally, he got back on track. "But they all take time, and this last week has been really hectic, as you can imagine with all the complaints. I really haven't had time to work on any other ideas. We'll get the new flyers out and get this trial program behind us, and that will give me time to concentrate on my next haircut …uh, I mean, idea."

Jonathan couldn't help but close his eyes and shake his head in disbelief. *This man is not a leader, but a freeloader, and his entire department has been carried on the back of the sales department for years.*

"Good, Cliff. I just hope your next haircut is better than your last," Charles chuckled.

Cliff didn't catch the humor, as he stroked his hair for anything out of place. Wanting to seem in tune, he began laughing with the group, though a little embarrassed.

"I guess those items pretty much cover the crux of our meeting. Looking ahead, we should be able to give an answer in about another three weeks as to whether we will be able to have any wage increases this year. Lisa, as discussed last week, you're prepared to handle that, correct?"

"Yes, Mr. Gantly."

"Lou, it's good to see you back."

"Thank you, Mr. Gantly, it's good to be back."

"Does anyone have anything else to add?" The room was quiet.

Jonathan raised his hand to garner Charles's attention. "Charles," he called. "I have made significant progress in recent days toward solidifying a successful sales marketing strategy. I'm not fully prepared to go into all the details at this time; however, I'd like to have a meeting Monday morning at 8:45 with everyone in this room. I have an exciting announcement, and you don't want to miss it."

"Sounds like this may be worth getting up early for," Charles replied. "I guess we'll see you then, Jonathan. That's all I have, folks. Thank you for your help."

Jonathan was the first to exit the room. Everyone else stood and began filing out the door, with Cliff and Ray dragging behind. "I see you got a haircut," Cliff said. "Did you go see Bruno?"

"Yeah. Great guy. It's a great place for a man to get a haircut or just catch up on his reading. He has all kinds of magazines, even for the construction trade. Have you ever heard of The Earth Movers and Shakers?"

"I have. That's a great magazine."

"This month's addition was chock full of neat ideas and strategies," Ray said with a suspicious smile.

Cliff stood speechless. "I better get going," he replied, and turned to walk away.

"I hope, next time, you do get a better haircut," Ray called out. Cliff turned back around.

"My next idea will be better than the first," he began to explain. "You see, I'm working on a new—"

"No," Ray interrupted, "I mean you really do need a better haircut." Ray walked off, leaving Cliff standing there with a bewildered look, combing his hair with his hands.

Tom finished up with his last appointment for the morning and headed off to his noon interview at McCardy's, where he was ushered to table 24. Upon his arrival, Paul stood to meet him and introduced himself. "Paul Grissom." He offered his hand to Tom.

"Mr. Grissom. Tom Brandent. I'm glad to meet you."

"Please, have a seat." It had been a long time since Tom had been in the position of interviewing for a job, but it felt good, though he was a little uncomfortable.

Their server approached the table just as they both sat down. "Hello, gentlemen, my name is Myra and I'll be your server this afternoon. What can I get you two to drink?" she asked, looking toward Tom.

"I'll have iced tea."

"And for you, sir?" she directed to Paul.

"I'll have tea, also, thank you."

"Are you gentlemen ready to order, or do you need a couple of minutes?"

Paul had been perusing his menu before Tom arrived, but had not made up his mind yet, though he was ninety percent settled on his favorite selection. Tom raised his menu, but just for a brief moment, as he had already made up his mind before he arrived at the restaurant.

"Tom, if you've never been here, I can honestly recommend anything on the menu. It's all good stuff."

"Oh, I know. I've been here many times and love the steaks."

"It sounds like you've already made up your mind," Paul said smiling.

"I have. But if you need a few minutes."

"Oh, no. Go ahead and order. I'll have my mind made up by the time you're through."

"Okay," Tom replied. Looking to Myra, "I'll have the rib-eye, cooked medium well, with a baked potato and house salad."

159

Tom handed her his menu.

"And for you, sir?" she directed to Paul.

"I'll have the catfish platter, dinner portion," he responded, and handed her his menu.

"Thank you, I'll have this right out." Myra turned and walked away.

"Tom, I want to thank you for agreeing to meet with me on such short notice."

"No problem," Tom responded, as he sat back in his seat. "Besides, changing schedules is part of being a salesman."

"You've got that right," Paul admitted. "I'd like to tell you a little about us, which you're probably more familiar with than you realize, but first, I'd like to hear what it is you're looking for and why you can't get it at Gantly."

This is your opportunity, and you need to get it right; there is no second chance for a first impression. "I've been with Gantly for over six years, and I love my job. I like meeting new people and helping them solve problems by providing products they can use. I've been around equipment all my professional career, and I've grown to love it, so I'd like to continue in this field. At Gantly, we carry a wide range of offerings, comparable to our competition, and very price competitive." Tom stopped short and closed his eyes, a little embarrassed, as he recognized he had gotten off on a tangent. *Where did that come from? Stay focused!*

"It sounds like you're not really sure if you want to leave."

"I'm sorry, Mr. Grissom, I'm just a little nervous. There's no doubt I want to leave. In fact, if this meeting doesn't pan out, I'm going to continue to search until I find something that will."

"May I ask what it is that's driving you away?"

Tom hesitated before responding; *I was hoping to get through this without mentioning Jonathan.* "It's my supervisor," he admitted. "I don't mind having a boss that will motivate me to do better or sell more, to encourage me, or even reprimand me when I need it; however, my supervisor has gotten to the point of harassing and belittling me, thinking that's going to motivate me. I don't

160

like being boastful, Mr. Grissom, but I'm doing a great job, bringing in about forty percent of the gross dollars in equipment sales for the company."

Myra came back with their drink order, interrupting Tom's response, and Paul sat back to be out of her way. "Here are your drinks, gentlemen." She set their glasses down. "Your food order will be out in just a few minutes."

"Thank you," they both said, as she walked away.

"Tom, it sounds like you've reached the end of your rope at Gantly," he said, as he added sugar to his tea.

"I really have, Mr. Grissom. I've decided to leave Gantly, and God has given me perfect peace about it ever since."

"Oh, are you a Christian, Tom?"

"Yes, I am. I accepted Christ as my Savior many years ago."

"Great! So am I."

"I wasn't the best example of a Christian for a long time, but I've grown a lot spiritually in the last year or so and have tried to let God work His perfect will in my life. I've prayed about this decision for a long time and His peace enables me to move on and put Gantly behind me."

"That's the most important part of the decision," Paul acknowledged, as he sampled his tea. "You certainly don't want to go any further than you already have while looking back."

"I'm not going to look back on this decision, that's for sure. There's a place out there for me somewhere, and I know God will lead me to it." Tom paused as he ran through a mental list of topics, to be sure he covered the important ones. Satisfied he had, "I guess I've about covered everything on my side."

"Good!" Paul leaned forward. "Let me tell you a little about our company and go from there. First, I am the sales manager for Landover, your biggest competition." Tom was shocked, but pleasantly surprised, and his facial expression told Paul the same thing. "As you are aware, we sell basically the same style equipment as Gantly, with the added benefit of a much larger service shop. As you are also aware, our company had not been known for having an overly productive sales force until recently, about the last two years, during which time, we have seen phenomenal growth. We just recently completed some major facility renovations that consolidated many of our groups that had been scattered all over our property. We expanded our service shop and our production area. All in all, these latest renovations have positioned us to be a major player in this business for many years to come." Tom could hear the excitement in Paul's voice—an excitement he had not felt at Gantly since before Malcolm.

"That all sounds pretty impressive."

"The one thing we're missing is another equipment salesman, which is why you and I are meeting today. I can't tell you how pleased I was to see your name show up on our list of positive prospects." Tom looked surprised. "In fact, I thought you were so comfortable at Gantly that I had asked Austin to take your name off the call list after the last time you turned us down. Thankfully, he forgot."

Tom was convinced God had brought this all together. "Mr. Grissom, I know I can do the job, and would appreciate the opportunity to show you!"

"There's no question in my mind you can do the job. I would never have setup an impromptu meeting like this with anyone I wasn't sure about. I'm aware of your capabilities and work ethic, and I've met several mutual customers that speak highly of you. To be honest with you, I've waited a long time for the opportunity to meet you under these circumstances."

"Thank you for the kind words, Mr. Grissom," Tom replied.

"You're welcome, but you deserve them. I believe you could be a great asset to our sales group and would like to extend an offer to you to come work with us." Tom sat astonished. His mouth dropped open, and his eyes lit up.

"Mr. Grissom," Tom fumbled out of his mouth as he gathered himself, "as I said earlier, I'd love to come to work for you!"

"May I take that as an official affirmative response?" Paul

asked, smiling, while sitting back in his seat.

"Yes, sir!"

"Then let me offer you this." Paul removed a letter from his shirt pocket and handed it to Tom. "That's an official offer letter from Landover. I wanted to be fully prepared for this possibility, and I'm glad I was."

Tom unfolded the letter and read it over. It was short and to the point. The base salary was more than he was making at Gantly and the sales bonus had greater potential. He couldn't help but to be overwhelmed with this good fortune, as he shook his head. Paul's smile disappeared.

"Not enough?" he asked.

"Oh, no, no, Mr. Grissom, everything's fine. God has been good to me to bring this all together, as undeserving as I am."

"God has been good to me, too, in answering my prayer for a new salesman. Do you have any questions?"

"When do I start?"

"When you tell your supervisor you've accepted another sales position with a competitor, you know your role as a salesman will almost demand that your employer let you go immediately."

"I understand, Mr. Grissom," Tom admitted. "And I wouldn't blame them. I fully expect to be dismissed upon my announcement. In fact, to avoid any conflict of interest, I will probably leave on my own once I submit my resignation."

"Then the answer to your question is you can start any day. What about Monday?"

"To be honest, Mr. Grissom, I have appointments that will keep me out of the office all this afternoon. I'll not have an opportunity to meet with my supervisor until sometime Monday morning. But I'll turn in my resignation as soon as I can and see how it goes."

"Fair enough. I'll just wait to hear from you. But come on over once you're free."

"Thanks, Mr. Grissom." The negotiations were sealed with a handshake, just as Myra brought their food.

"Gentlemen, "here's your lunch."

She sat Tom's steak in front of him, with the baked potato and house salad. "Man, this looks good, as usual."

"Wait till you see this catfish platter."

Myra sat the large platter in front of Paul, and Tom's eyes opened wide. "Wow!" Tom said. "I've never had that before!"

"This is what I'm talking about," Paul commented, as he began to arrange his plate. "You'll soon learn I'm all about lunch. It's important that we all succeed at our jobs, but it's just as important that we have a good lunch."

"Amen to that," Tom added. "I'm also a lunch aficionado."

"What a pair we are," Paul suggested. "Let's pray and thank God for His goodness."

It was 2:00pm and the day was going by fast for Daniel. He had spent almost all morning out in the shop trying to help with a major repair on a machine required to be on a job site the following Tuesday morning. After resolving the problem, returning several phone calls, and updating his maintenance schedule, he noticed it was already past lunch and he had not eaten yet. He went down the hallway and bought a few things from the vending machines and kept working, hoping he would get caught up, but he knew better. He remembered he had promised Tom he would call to let him know how it went with his dad. Tom had just left a customer's facility, and he was on the highway when his cell phone rang.

"This is Tom. How may I help you?"

"Hey, Tom, it's Daniel. I wanted to call you earlier to tell you how it went with my dad, but it's been a busy day."

"I understand. So how did it go?"

"It turns out my dad is on top of our situation, the big debt and all, and what it's going to take to get it all paid for. He says he has a plan that will get us out of debt pretty quickly, or at least much quicker than the bank loan."

"That sounds like a very aggressive plan, Daniel. He's probably planning to sell your largest machine like we had discussed and take a hit on it to substantially reduce his debt. It's not the best news, but it's better than the alternative."

"Oh, no. He's not going to sell anything."

"You mean he's going to keep all the equipment?"

"You bet," Daniel responded. "A Torres does not go back on his word," Daniel said, changing his voice trying to impersonate his father.

"What does that mean?" Tom asked.

"That's what my dad said. He says that since we made the original deal, we need to stick with all the original terms. We agreed to buy the equipment, so we will."

"But, Daniel," Tom argued, trying to be polite, "I don't think …" Tom hesitated before continuing. "Just a moment." He pulled off the street and into a nearby parking lot to be able to offer his full attention. "Daniel, please hear me out," Tom admonished. "I am not an accountant, but I have been trained in accounting. I am not a banker, but I have been involved in many loans and financial negotiations. From my perspective, and take it for what it's worth, something is not adding up."

"What do you mean."

"When given all the parameters of this deal, the math works out to be what it is. To make any appreciable change in the existing contractual terms would take either a major reduction in debt, maybe by selling the large machine, or a major influx of cash from wherever."

"I know he's not going to sell anything," Daniel stated, "and I don't think we have any rich relatives."

Tom paused a moment, while he closed his eyes and considered the circumstances. *Lord, please give me wisdom for Daniel and help us both understand the situation better.* "It sounds like your dad is a mighty proud man."

"Oh, yes," Daniel affirmed. "He'd rather die than tell anyone he made a bad deal. It totally shocked me last night when my dad said Jack Fisher was a better salesman than he was a businessman."

Finally, Tom thought. *Now we're getting somewhere.* "It sounds like Albert knows he made a bad deal."

"My dad wouldn't make a bad deal," he snapped.

"I'm not saying he would, Daniel, and certainly not on purpose. I'm just saying, in my opinion, this deal has no good outcome unless something dramatic happens to change the situation."

"What are you trying to say, Tom?"

"I'm not sure what I'm trying to say anymore, Daniel," Tom answered a little frustrated. "I know your dad wouldn't do anything like this on his own. Perhaps someone convinced him it was a good deal, maybe enticed him—I don't know! Look," he said, throwing in the towel, "maybe I'm just blowing this all out of proportion, as I've said before. You said your dad has a plan; perhaps we just need to have more faith in him to know what he's doing. Maybe he really can turn this around and make it all work out."

"Man, I'm afraid I don't know enough to be able to know what to think anymore. This emotional roller coaster I've been on the last few days has really got me all turned around. I feel like my dad was very open and honest with me last night, that he didn't hold anything back. He sounded so confident that he had it all under control."

"I don't know what your dad has planned, but I really hope it all works out for you guys," Tom said, a little more relaxed. "Albert has been in business for many years, and I'm sure he's seen his share of hard times."

"I have to believe my dad knows what he's doing and stand behind him when he does it," Daniel said. "After all, we're in this together."

"Now that's about the most logical thing I've heard concerning this matter," Tom agreed. "Let me know if there is anything I can do to help." Tom hung up the phone and prayed for Albert and Daniel. "Perhaps," he said, "I can be more help once I became an official Landover employee. For now, they'll have to work it out themselves, together."

Chapter 15

Albert got up early every morning, and this Saturday was no exception. As he finished his breakfast, he said to his wife, "I need to go to the office this morning."

"Now?" she asked.

"Yes. I have …something to do."

"But you haven't read the paper yet."

"The paper is overrated, and full of old news. We need to look forward to better things."

"Does this have anything to do with you ordering your special breakfast this morning and those fine clothes you have on?" she smiled. "I thought you may have had something special planned for us."

He reached over and grabbed her hand. "Every day is special with you, Rosa." He patted her hand and gave her a kiss.

"How long will you be gone?"

"If I'm not back in a couple of hours you can come looking for me," he jested.

It was a short, fifteen-minute drive in his big, shiny, brand-new truck, maybe eight miles, and with no one else at the shop, Albert parked close to the front door. He sat in his truck for a moment, thinking of the old, rundown pickup he owned when he first started his company, and how things had changed since then. He removed his keys, exited the vehicle, and clicked his remote to set the alarm. The only alarm he had on his first truck was the sympathy of any perspective thief, to realize Albert needed his truck, and the things in it, more than the thief did.

Before approaching the building, Albert stood in the parking lot admiring the facilities he had managed to assemble during his business career. He remembered when the front office area was an old three-bedroom house and the workshop was a two-car garage, and it was all in need of repairs when he first bought it. Renovations were made in the early years as funds allowed, which eventually produced a reasonably comfortable office area and a spacious workshop with all the necessary tooling for machine repairs and maintenance. Having started with just two employees—Albert and his wife—Torres Construction now had thirty-five people on the payroll.

Albert unlocked the front door, turned off the alarm, and entered the lobby area, locking the door behind him. He stood and gazed at all the items on the walls: job-site pictures, business awards, and special gifts of appreciation. Each of them spoke volumes about the history of Torres Construction, and Albert could remember it all. From the purchase of the original building, their first contract, the first new tractor, the birth of his son, to hiring his son to work with him. "These are all great memories," he said, as he reached to touch the photo of Daniel with his first official paycheck. Albert nodded his head at each of these achievements, then lifting his head high, he walked to his office, stopping in Daniel's office long enough to lay an envelope on his desk.

In his office doorway, he stopped once again to reflect on days gone by, to take in all the memories the room had to offer. He could remember the plumbing that had to be removed to allow the expansion of his office, and the hardwood floors that had since been covered with carpeting. Larger windows had been installed to bring in some much-needed sunlight, allowing a much larger view of the outside scenery to offer a mental escape when the job pressures were too great. The area did not offer the greatest of window views, but it beat staring all day at a mound of paperwork on his desk. Starting on his left, he walked around the office perimeter, observing and touching almost everything along his way with special reflection. Each wall-hung memento had a special significance and Albert seemed to try to relive all those memories as he made his way around the room.

Reaching the back side of his office, he opened one of the window blinds, gazed outside for a few moments, and then closed it back. He closed his eyes to gather his resolve, breathing in through his nose and out his mouth, blowing out the last deep breath like an athlete psyched for competition. With stern determination, Albert walked to his desk and took a seat. He removed the document from his coat pocket, laid it on his desk, and once again reviewed the highlighted areas he and Tony had gone over a few days earlier. He was confident he had understood his brother's explanation, regarding Albert's terminally ill friend. Tony had been in the business for over thirty years and assured Albert his friend's family had nothing to worry about.

"I guess I'm legal," Albert said. He folded the document and put it off to the side. His heart was pounding away, as he opened the upper-right desk drawer and removed a decorative, wooden display box. The gift card was still on top, and Albert read it again. "Pull the trigger and make the deal. Signed, Jack Fisher." He snickered at the irony. "If he only knew." He tossed the card onto his desk and set the box in front of him.

He raised the ornate lid to reveal a shiny, black, nine-millimeter with ivory grips and fancy, pearl inlay. "A beautiful thing," he said, "but beauty must often be sacrificed for a greater good." Next to his desk nameplate sat a picture of his wife. Albert raised the picture to his mouth, kissed it, and then laid it face down on his desk.

With all the strength he could muster, he reached for the gun. His fingertips could feel every edge of the cold steel as he brushed his hand along the length of the barrel. He felt along the outline of the gun for the release tab that secured the gun in the display case and, pressing it, managed to pull the gun loose from its recessed cutout. He firmly gripped the smooth handle and withdrew it from its velvet-lined pocket, his hand shaking and his heart rate increasing the more. Albert had handled a few firearms in his lifetime, but none had seemed quite as heavy as the one he was holding now, weighted down with the business pressures and financial burdens he felt strapped with. He was careful to leave his finger off the trigger to keep from pulling it before its time—something he had learned from Daniel's instructions. The temperature in his office was a comfortable seventy-two degrees, but the tension alone was enough to cover his brow with sweat, while his lower jaw began to shake, and his eyes were blinking almost at the same rate. He squeezed his eyes closed as he raised the gun toward his head, using the cold sensation of the barrel against his skin as a guide to let him know when he had it in the proper location. He felt it brush his ear as it jittered along the side of his face, moving into position. His hand still shaking, he pressed the barrel against his temple to keep it from moving around. He gritted his teeth and clenched his jaws tight, causing his neck muscles to stand out. Everything was ready. He tried to decide when to pull the trigger, as he counted from one to three several times on top of each successive exhale. Every time he decided on which number to pull the trigger, he would change his mind. First three, then two, then three again. He seemed to always have an excuse as to why he did not pull the trigger: he was not ready, he did not say the number loud enough, his hand moved, he forgot the number, or he miscounted.

After about two long, grueling minutes of indecisiveness and uncertainty, Albert lost his concentration and stopped counting. He relaxed his jaw and neck muscles then opened his eyes. His hand was no longer shaking. He moved the gun away from his head, and rested his hand on the desktop, releasing the gun from his grip. He sat motionless for a moment then scanned the room to be sure nothing had changed—all was in order; he was still alone. Exhausted, he folded his arms on the desktop and collapsed on top of them, weeping aloud. As the weeping subsided, he soon found himself chuckling before bursting out into a full uncontrollable laughter. He raised his head and cupped his hands over his face as he took a couple of deep breaths, and then broke out in heavy laughter once again. He reached for a tissue and wiped his eyes. After a few more unsuccessful attempts to stop laughing, he gathered his composure, as he sat back in his chair with his eyes closed and continued his deep breathing. Emotionally drained, he leaned forward, reached for his wife's picture, and set it back up. "I can't do this to you, Rosa," he said, looking at the picture with tears streaming down his cheeks. "Besides," he continued, as he remembered with a smile, "I never bought any ammunition for the gun." He laughed again.

He slumped back, all the way, into his chair and rested for a few minutes to relax his muscles. "You idiot!" he said, covering his face with his hands. "Of all the stupid and selfish things I've done, this would have been the worst." He opened his mouth several times while he rubbed his jaw joints, trying to relieve the muscle ache. Feeling his strength replenish, he sat up and leaned forward, as he stared at the pistol. "God," he said, his lips trembling, "if you can hear me, and if this was your doing, I don't know why you stopped me, but I'm glad you did, even though I don't deserve it." He wiped away his tears, put away the gun, and closed his desk drawer. "Daniel, I guess we," he closed his eyes as he corrected himself, "I, need to swallow my pride and do what is best for all of us."

Albert reached for his desk calendar and laid it in front of him. He had made a note a few weeks back on today's date to give him encouragement, which simply read, Debt Free. He took his pen, scratched through the note, and wrote below it, Not Worth It. "It's about time I realize there is more to life than the material things a man owns or owes, no matter their value." He placed the calendar back on his desk and sat and cried for a few moments, relieved that the hard part was all over.

Albert stood to his feet, straightened his jacket, and said, "A Torres does not run from a fight. A Torres finishes what he starts." He held his head up high as he walked out of his office and to the lobby, where he reset the alarm and exited the building, locking the door behind him.

In the parking lot, he glanced down at his watch and realized he had been gone much longer than the two hours he had told his wife. "She's going to kill me," he said, as he hurried on home.

Friday evening was a time of rejoicing at the Brandent house, as Linda was pleased to hear the announcement of Tom's new job. It was an answer to prayer for both, and a much-needed change for Tom.

By early Saturday morning the excitement had not subsided, and Tom couldn't wait to tell Chris. He stirred around the house as long as he could to be sure Chris would be up before heading over to see him, preferring to deliver the news in person. He arrived about 9:30am and Dana answered the door. "Hi, Dana. I need to talk with Chris if he's in."

"Sure. He's out back working in the yard." She invited Tom in and escorted him to the back door. Dana opened the back patio door and yelled, "Chris, Tom is here to see you!"

"Be there in a minute!" he answered, laying down his tree trimmer.

"Can I get you something to drink, Tom?" Dana asked, as Tom stepped outside.

"Oh no, I'm fine, thank you." She stepped back inside and closed the patio door.

As Chris made his way to the patio, he removed his gloves and wiped his face off with his towel. "Hey, Tom," he greeted, "what's up?"

"I was going to call before I came over, but I thought I'd just surprise you. If you've got a few minutes, I'd like to talk."

"Sure. I was about to take a break anyway. Have a seat," gesturing to the familiar patio furniture.

They each took a seat at the table by the pool. Chris set his gloves and towel out of their way.

"I finally did it," Tom started. "I'm leaving Gantly," he announced, and waited for Chris's response.

Chris paused a moment, as if waiting for something else, and then responded, "Tom, you've already told me that. I know you want to leave Gantly."

"No! I mean I'm leaving soon. I've been offered a new job."

"Wow!" Chris reeled back in his chair. "I knew it would happen eventually but not this fast. Man! Are you sure about this?"

"I've never been surer about anything."

"Who offered you the job?"

"You won't believe this." Tom was getting more excited as he spoke with Chris. "You remember when you and I talked about this last Saturday, we both knew it would probably be with a competitor?"

"Yeah, I remember."

"I got a phone call the other day from a headhunter and he arranged a meeting between me and his client for lunch yesterday; that's why I couldn't have lunch with you. I wanted to tell you what was going on, but I thought it was a little premature before our meeting."

"That's fine. I understand. I wouldn't have said anything either if it was me."

"We met at McCardy's."

"Ooh, nice," Chris said.

"Yeah, it was."

174

"What'd you have to eat?"

"Come on, let me finish; besides, the catfish platter is another story, but it is something we need to try the next time we're there! Anyway, you'll never guess who I met with." Chris shrugged his shoulders. "Paul Grissom."

Chris sat for a moment, unable to conjure an image or memory. "Who's Paul Grissom?" he said, throwing out his hands.

"Oh, I'm sorry. Before yesterday, I didn't know who he was either. Paul Grissom is the sales manager for Landover."

"Landover, aye." Chris was excited for Tom, as they all suspected Landover had a nice facility, based on what they had seen from the roadway on their occasional drive-bys. "So, you might be going to Landover?"

"No might to it," he said. "I am going! We talked for a while and Mr. Grissom handed me an offer letter at the table."

Chris sat up and his eyes widened. "What'd you tell him?"

"I told him yes and accepted his offer!" he said with a big smile.

"That's great! When do you start?"

"I'm offering my letter of resignation to Jonathan on Monday, if he'll talk to me. He's told me before, if I ever decide to resign, to turn in my resignation and leave—he doesn't want to discuss it. I'm still going to offer it to him personally. It's the least I can do to be professional about it."

"What does Linda think about all this?"

"She's more excited than I am. She told me she could tell I was letting Jonathan's attitude affect me, and it was about time I made a change."

"You know I'll certainly miss you at work, and our Friday lunches."

"I'll miss it all, too, but this is an opportunity I can't refuse. I believe God has opened this door and it's His will I walk through it. Besides, we'll still be able to meet for lunch occasionally."

"It's all a little bitter-sweet, but I totally understand," Chris assured him. He patted Tom on the shoulder. "I wish you the best, and hope it all works out for you, as I'm sure it will."

"Thanks for your support, Chris. I talked to Linda last night about this and couldn't wait to let you know. I guess I'd better be going and let you get back to your yard work."

"Thanks for coming by and giving me the update. I guess we'll see each other at work on Monday, at least for a little while, and I'll be praying the transition will go smooth."

It was great to have a friend like Chris. Tom knew his own family would support and encourage him in whatever he felt led to do—though he was careful to not take it for granted—but to have a friend that would do the same was priceless.

Chapter 16

Daniel whistled a catchy tune as he arrived to work early Monday morning, the cool breeze hardly noticeable under his light, long overcoat. He snapped up the newspaper from the dew-covered lawn and shook off what little moisture had gathered on the plastic wrap before entering the building and turning off the alarm. The typical morning ritual started in the kitchen with a fresh pot of coffee. While the coffee brewed, he carried the newspaper to his office doorway and tossed it onto his desk. When he turned to leave, something on his desk caught his eye. He walked into his office, picked up the newspaper, and saw an envelope lying underneath addressed to him. He picked up the envelope, set the newspaper back down on his desk, and withdrew the rather lengthy letter that was inside. He immediately recognized his father's handwriting. "Oh, Dad, you didn't have to apologize." He began reading.

Dear Daniel: By the time you read this I will have done a most awful deed. Please forgive me, as there was no other way.

Daniel was smiling inside. It took a lot of courage for his father to apologize for anything.

Someday I hope you will look back on this and know that I did it all for you and your mother. In these pages, I have left behind detailed instructions to handle the business and some special notes for your mother.

Daniel grew worried, sensing this was more than an apology and was afraid of what may have already taken place.

I am a very proud man, and don't know how to humble myself, but I can be brave in a letter. I was wrong, but rather than let you see my humility, I have decided to take my life. Only a fool would have fallen for Jack Fisher's offer, and I am that fool, but I believe that my—

He threw the pages down and ran to his father's office and turned on the light. Not finding what he expected, he ran over to his father's desk and called his parents' home. While he waited for someone to answer, he noticed the life insurance policy Albert had left behind. He unfolded the pages and noticed the specific areas highlighted. "Hello," his mother answered.

"Hey, Mom, is Dad around?" he asked, trying to remain calm.

"Yes, Daniel, but he's about to leave for work. Is everything okay?"

"Oh sure, Mom, everything is fine," Daniel answered. "I just need to talk to Dad for a minute."

She called Albert to the phone. "Hello, Daniel," Albert answered.

"Dad, I came to the office this morning and found an envelope on my desk."

"Uh, yes, Daniel, don't open it," Albert cautioned in a low voice.

"Too late, Dad, I already have. What is this about?" Daniel asked, as he continued to search Albert's desk for other clues.

Albert waited until his wife had left the room before responding. "I'll explain it all to you when I get to work. Okay?"

Then Daniel found the gift card Albert left out on his desk. "But, Dad, Jack Fisher started this. Why didn't you tell me what was going on?"

"Daniel, please. I'll explain it all when I get to work. Promise me you won't do anything until I get there. I'm on my way." Albert hung up the phone and rushed out the door.

Continuing to scour Albert's desktop for more clues, Daniel noticed the hand-written entries on Albert's desktop calendar. Debt Free, Not Worth It. He opened the top-right desk drawer and noticed the special gift box, which he removed, placed on the desktop, and opened the lid. "You've got to be kidding me," he said, staring at the gun. "And for what!" he chided. "Money? Really, Dad. You thought this would fix everything?" Putting it all together: the letter, the gift card, the insurance policy, the vacation, the gun, and the calendar notes; Daniel surmised his father had been pushed to the brink of committing an awful deed. The more he thought of what could have been, the angrier he became. "Pull the trigger, huh. I'll pull Jack Fisher's trigger."

By now, Janet had arrived and was getting her first cup of coffee. She had noticed Albert's office light was on but did not think anything about it, since she knew Daniel was there. With her cup in hand, she started to her workstation and was only able to see a glimpse of Daniel as he darted through the lobby and out the front door.

"Hey, Daniel," she called, but he was already to the parking lot. "I wonder where he's going in such a hurry."

Jonathan arrived to work on Monday morning with a spring in his step and a new song in his heart over his latest feat of hiring Jack Fisher. Finally, Jonathan had a man on staff that would follow his every lead and close sales like no one before, with exception to Jonathan himself, of course. He knew this achievement could be a real boost to his bid to be President of Gantly someday, possibly grand enough to convince Charles to retire a few years early.

He stepped lively as he walked through the front door, carrying some special breakfast snacks to share with the rest of the staff. These were not just ordinary donuts, but delicate pastries and fruit-bread muffins—an assortment to please any palate. Thankfully, there were very few people at the office when Jonathan arrived, so the pleasant aroma was not detected by anyone else's snack radar right away. He was able to make it to the boardroom without being noticed, where he closed the door behind him to be sure he would not be disturbed, and he set the snacks on the table. He arranged the chairs around the table to give every attendee the best view of the area where he would be making his presentation and formal introduction of Jack. In Jonathan's opinion, hiring Jack Fisher would shift the local industrial sales market to such a degree that he had to prepare some special flip charts representing his vision of Gantly's grand future in the newly aligned equipment marketplace.

Tom arrived to work right at 8:00am, with two copies of his resignation letter in his pocket—one for Jonathan and one for Lisa, to be sure his resignation was delivered to the proper personnel. He entered the front door and stopped in the lobby to reminisce of his years at Gantly, looking around at all the scenery, remembering all the good and bad times. "Good morning, Tom. Are you lost?" Claire asked, as Tom stood motionless and looked out of sorts.

Tom caught himself and looked over at Claire. "Oh, no. I was just thinking," he said as he walked to his office. "And good morning to you, too, Claire."

After entering his office, Tom sat at his desk, knowing it would probably be for the last time, using the opportunity to assure himself of the reality of what was about to happen, as it all seemed so surreal now. He had rehearsed this scene in his mind a thousand times—what he would say, how he would act, how he would feel—but now it was time to perform. His years at Gantly had been great, but he knew it was time to move on.

Jonathan usually had his first cup of coffee before Tom

arrived, so Tom decided to spring the news on him right away. After a moment of self-reflection, he rose from his desk with his letter in hand and made his way to Jonathan's office. Passing by Chris' office, he looked in as Chris gave him the thumbs-up sign, which Tom returned with a smile and a slight nod. Arriving at Jonathan's doorway, he was a little disappointed to not find him in. Standing there, he glanced up to notice Jonathan exiting the boardroom, walking toward his office. Tom prepared himself as Jonathan approached him.

"Good morning, Jonathan," Tom greeted.

"Good morning, Tom," Jonathan replied in a real chipper tone, continuing into his office without so much as looking in Tom's direction.

"Jonathan, have you got a minute?" Tom asked, as he followed Jonathan into his office.

"Not right now, Tom, I'm very busy." He marched straight to his desk, shuffled through some papers on top, and took the ones he needed to help with his presentation.

"But this is really important," Tom pleaded, as he followed Jonathan back out of his office and into the hallway.

Jonathan stopped in the hallway to offer a patronizing stare. "I'm sure it is, Tom, and I'm really very interested in hearing it." then turning to make his way back to the boardroom, "But not now."

"But, Jonathan," Tom called out, as Jonathan continued walking, "I'm about to leave and I have a letter for you. It will explain everything."

"Do whatever you think you need to do," he said, without missing a step or turning around. "Give the letter to Claire and I'll read it later. If I have any questions, I'll call you on your cell phone." he said, raising his arm and gesturing a backward wave.

Tom stood in the hallway, having just been reminded once again why he was leaving. He decided he would go pack his things and follow Jonathan's advice, to give the letter to Claire and leave. On his way back to his office he stopped to see Chris, who heard the verbal exchange.

"Man, that guy is a piece of work," Tom commented, as he walked into Chris' office.

"Oh, don't mind him. He's in a frenzy trying to get ready for that big, important meeting he called with Charles's staff. Look at the bright side; this is your last day with him. Not to mention the fact you're going to leave him in a bad mood once he reads your letter, and then I'll have to put up with him."

"It couldn't happen to a nicer guy," Tom joked.

"So, what are you going to do now, since he won't talk to you?"

"I guess I'll just go back to my office, pack my things, and leave. I can't force my supervisor to stop and listen to me, and I feel guilty to sit around here waiting for him to have time for me." Tom thought for a moment. "There are several people I'd like to say goodbye to, but I don't think Mr. Gantly would approve. I'm sure he'd rather have Jonathan know before everybody else."

"I'll be sure to let everyone know you wanted to, once word gets out about your resignation."

"Thanks, Chris. Hey, I know we can't do this every week, but let's have lunch this Friday."

"That sounds great."

"I guess I'd better get out of here. I'll see you Friday."

"See you then. Be careful out there."

"And you do the same," Tom replied, as he turned and left Chris' office.

It didn't take Tom very long to pack, as he had decided a long time ago to remove most all his personal possessions, with exception to a few family photos, books, and mementos. He gathered his things in one small box, taped it shut, and decided to walk it out to his car before giving his letters to Claire. He had often carried boxes out for various customers, and no one ever took notice. But today he felt a little awkward, almost guilty, hoping his actions would not draw any attention.

With the package secured in his car, Tom made his way back to his office to leave his company-issued property: cell phone, identification badge, and credit card. While laying these things on his desk, he noticed something different about his office. He looked back toward his doorway, and it finally dawned on him. He closed his eyes and grinned.

He walked down to Chris's office as all the managers were headed to the boardroom to get an early start on the snacks Jonathan brought. He stopped at the doorway and looked in at Chris.

"Boy, that didn't take long." Tom stood at his doorway and waited for a response.

"What?" Chris asked, grinning ear to ear and stretching his arms out as if he had nothing to hide.

"Couldn't you have at least waited until my car was out of the parking lot?" Tom asked, pointing at his old coatrack, now in Chris' office.

"Just trying to beat the office-furniture buzzards."

"Alright, buddy. I'll see you."

Tom left Chris and started out for the last time. He stopped at Claire's desk and handed her the two, individually addressed envelopes. "Claire, would you see that Lisa and Jonathan get these when they get out of their meeting, please?"

"Sure, Tom," she replied, as Tom headed for the front door. "You headed out?"

"Yep, I'm headed out."

"Do you have any idea when you'll be back?" Claire wanted to be sure she kept her office attendance schedule updated.

Tom stopped and posed, as though giving deep thought to the question. "I sure don't Claire," he replied. "I have no idea."

"Have a good day."

"You, too, Claire." Tom paused at the door. Looking back, he said, "You do a great job, Claire, and you always have," and then exited the building. Now it was off to his new employer.

A few minutes after Tom walked out, Jonathan went to the

lobby and stopped at Claire's desk. "Claire, I am expecting a young man, Jack Fisher, to be here at 9:00am sharp. Please let me know when he arrives."

"Yes, sir, Mr. Edwards." Then, remembering Tom's letter as Jonathan turned to leave, "Mr. Edwards."

"Yes, Claire," he turned back and answered.

"There's a letter here for you from Tom Brandent."

"Yes, he told me he left it. I'll get it later. Thank you." He turned and made his way back to the boardroom.

Jack arrived at Landover just after 8:00am to be able to gather the remainder of his possessions and make it to Gantly before 9:00am. It was a thirty-minute drive, so he knew he had to hurry with his things and be on his way. Cheryl had walked away from her desk momentarily and did not see him come in, though Paul had told her to expect him. The other salesmen were in their Monday-morning meeting, so Jack was unencumbered as he made his way to his office with a small box. Looking around, he noticed the office vultures had already confiscated several sundry items, including the stapler and tape dispenser he used, which he had taken from the last salesman that left Landover. He gathered his last few mementos off the walls, personal toiletry items from his desk drawer, and several assorted paperweights he kept on his desk.

Jack wanted to say goodbye to a few of his coworkers but wasn't sure how he would be received under the circumstances, as word of his firing had spread throughout the company. After all, he had compromised the trust others had put in him and obligated Landover to cover his shady financial deals. Knowing he needed to get going, Jack decided to leave without speaking to anyone. He walked through the lobby, keeping his head down and avoiding making eye contact with Cheryl, who had made it back to her desk. His shame would not even allow him to say goodbye to her. Cheryl was speechless as he walked out the front door.

It was a short walk to his car, but today it felt so very long, as Jack left Landover for the last time. Thoughts of his many friendships he had developed at Landover raced through his mind, as he tried to assess the fallout from his shenanigans and wondered if they would survive. He seemed to be making forward progress on his surrealistic trek with only every-other step, as he drew closer to his destination. The burden he felt from what he had done was so great, even the small box he carried slowed him down.

At Torres Construction, Albert had just arrived at work. He ran into the office, where he met Janet at the front desk. She noticed he seemed concerned. "Good morning, Albert. It looks like you're in a hurry."

"Janet, have you seen Daniel?" Albert asked, as though he never heard her remarks. "I didn't see his car outside."

"I just saw him for a brief second when he bolted out the door as I was on my way back from the kitchen with my coffee."

"Did he say where he was going?"

"I didn't get a chance to ask. Is something wrong?"

Albert went to his office without answering her question. Once he entered, he could tell from the disheveled paperwork someone had been looking around. He went straight to his desk and opened his top-right drawer. Thankfully, the gift box was still there, but Albert picked it up to satisfy his curiosity. The light weight of the box caused his heart to jump, as he opened it to confirm the pistol was gone. "Oh no! Dear Lord, please don't let him do it!" he begged, as he ran to the lobby.

"Janet, how long ago did Daniel leave?"

"I think it was about fifteen or twenty minutes ago," she answered, almost to the point of tears.

Albert called Daniel's cell phone, hoping to persuade him to come back to the office, but he heard the familiar ringtone from the kitchen and realized Daniel had left it behind. Albert bolted out the door, knowing he needed to beat Daniel to Landover.

Jack tried to cheer himself up with the prospects of his new job, but things just weren't the same since the conversation with Bill. He knew Jonathan would expect a certain attitude, drive, and minimal level of work ethics, but wasn't sure he could deliver—not now. *I've got to toughen up. Jonathan needs me and I need this job.*

Cheryl watched Jack from the lobby as he walked across the parking lot, feeling a little sorry for him. Jerry walked up to the receptionist's desk with a cup of coffee in his hand and stared out the window at Jack. "So, I guess he's really gone," Jerry said, as he sipped his coffee.

"Yep," Cheryl replied. "I hope he gets along okay."

"Oh, he'll do fine. He just needs to keep his head up."

At that moment, Jack noticed a car pulling into the parking lot, as he stumbled and dropped his box of belongings.

"Great!" he snarled. "This is all I need."

"Whoa," Jerry said, as he saw Jack stumble.

"He's not off to a good start," Cheryl commented.

"I'd better look into getting that pothole fixed before someone gets seriously injured." He sipped his coffee as he looked across the parking lot. "Who's that?" Jerry asked Cheryl, as he gestured with a head nod toward the gentleman that exited the vehicle and headed over to Jack.

"I've never seen him before, but it looks like he may know Jack."

As Jack stooped down to gather his belongings, the man walked up in a long overcoat, hands in the pockets, and stopped in front of Jack, overshadowing him. Jack gave a quick glance to the one blocking the sunlight and recognized the figure above him. "Hey, Daniel, how's it going?" Jack asked, as he continued to gather his things, his thought process still a little numb to his surroundings. *Why is Daniel here? I need to get my things picked up.*

"Not so good, Jack, not so good," Daniel responded with a somber tone and straight face, as he stared down at Jack.

Jack paused for a moment to take a good look at Daniel's face and noticed he was a little distraught. "What's going on? Everything okay?" *I really need to get going. I don't want to be late.*

"I'm at a crossroad in my life and I need some advice."

"Is there anything I can do for you," Jack asked, while still retrieving his effects. *Please say no!*

"I think there is," Daniel began, continuing his sarcasm. "You're pretty good at persuasion. Perhaps you can guide me to what my next step should be."

"Next step?" A little confused, Jack left picking up his things and offered Daniel his full attention.

"You see," Daniel continued with a grimace, as he knelt beside Jack, "I need to figure out what to do with a low-down, gutless, snake. When we find them in the field, we usually just blow their heads off." He leaned in toward Jack. "What should I do with you?"

"Are you sure he knows Jack?" Jerry asked, noticing Daniel's mannerisms.

"I didn't say he knew Jack, I said it looked like he may know Jack."

"He looks a little aggressive to me," Jerry commented, as he set his coffee mug on the receptionist's counter, pulled his safety goggles from his pocket, and slipped them on. Once they were in place, he retrieved his coffee mug and took another drink. Cheryl looked over at him and did a double take.

Jack stood to his feet, disregarding his loose articles, and Daniel straightened up at the same time, never losing eye contact.

"Daniel, it sounds as though you're trying to make an accusation."

"No, Jack, I'm making an observation," he said. "An accusation needs to be proven, and I've seen all the proof I need to come to my conclusion that you are a snake. You're always looking for prey, you talk with a split tongue, and you use deception to your advantage. You, Jack, are a lying snake, and you lied to my father."

"Lies? What lies? I never lied to your father about anything. Perhaps there was just a misunderstanding," Jack suggested.

"The misunderstanding was you thinking no one would ever figure this out", Daniel said, as his lips grew tighter and his eyes smaller, while he stared at Jack, almost not blinking at all. "Do you realize my father mortgaged everything he had to purchase your equipment?"

"I assure you," Jack said, as he scrambled for words to fit together, holding his hands out as a token of innocence, "I discussed everything your father had questions about concerning the details of the agreement. There were no lies."

"That's just it," Daniel continued, his eyes widening, yet trying to keep his voice down to avoid drawing a crowd. "Your omission of the truth was your lies. You knew my father couldn't afford all the machinery, but you hounded him and hounded him until he gave in. You were so interested in helping him get credit approval, yet you couldn't have cared less about whether he would ever generate the revenue needed to pay it back. In your twisted mind, he got what he wanted, and you got what you wanted. In real terms, you got a commission check to fatten your wallet, and my father got a fat payment book he can't honor."

"It looks like Jack probably knows this guy," Cheryl said, "but their relationship appears to be a bit strained at the moment. Do you think I should call the police?" she asked, still staring from the window.

Bill walked into the lobby area with a concerned look on his face. He had been watching the event from his office window. "Do either of you know who that guy is talking to Jack?" Bill asked.

"I have no idea," Cheryl responded without turning around, "but he looks upset."

"I think he looks aggressive," Jerry chimed in while sipping his coffee and still staring out the window. Bill looked over at Jerry, noticed his safety goggles and did a double take before returning his attention to the incident outside. All three stood motionless and stared at the parking-lot confrontation.

Jack was speechless, unable to respond. He stood in silence with his hands dropped to his sides, realizing this encounter with Daniel was more planned than by chance. He moved his body about and tried to form his lips, hoping words would follow, but nothing. *What can I say? What is he going to do? I can't.... Why can't I think right now?* Daniel sharply broke the short silence.

"Remember what you gave my father, Jack, to help close your deal?" Jack remembered the gift, and his eyes drifted down from Daniel's face to the bulge in the right pocket of Daniel's long overcoat. "That's right, Jack, a nine-millimeter pistol," he said, his voice growing louder. "Forty-eight hours ago my father had planned to use your gracious gift to kill himself because of the shame he felt from getting in over his head financially with your ridiculous deal. I hold you personally responsible for bringing him to the point of contemplating such an act—a product of your egomaniacal, self-centered, manipulative approach."

This is not good, Jack thought. *Say something before he does something crazy!* But nothing followed.

Chapter 17

In the Gantly boardroom, Jonathan was prepared to start his meeting. As promised, Charles arrived earlier than normal to be on time, anxious to see what Jonathan had to present. Everyone enjoyed the breakfast snacks and was curious about what he was up to, as they began to settle down to hear his announcement. As the noise level diminished, Cliff leaned over and whispered to Ray, "Maybe he's retiring."

"No way," Ray responded. "People like Jonathan don't retire. They grow so old in the company that they eventually turn into a piece of office furniture."

"If I could have your attention, please," Jonathan began, as everyone got quiet, "I have a very important announcement to make. To the dismay of many," he quipped, "no, I'm not dying of a deadly disease or retiring." Everyone in the room laughed, most out of courtesy. "A few weeks ago, I embarked on a personal mission to generate new life into Gantly Industrial Sales to propel us to the forefront of all other businesses in our industry. I have searched high and low for the best talent with the ambition and drive to elevate us to the next level of market domination in our arena. My goal was to find an individual that knows our business, and how to use that knowledge to generate an unprecedented revenue stream for us. I wanted someone who could find a deal where others had been unsuccessful and close that deal before our competition knew it existed. Today, I have succeeded in this quest." Jonathan made his way over to the flip charts he had prepared. "I hope each of you took a few moments earlier this morning to go over these charts I put together. In each of them, I have used a blue marker to show where we would be if we continue our present downward spiral. The red marker indicates where I believe we are headed since acquiring our new asset. You may ask, can one man make such a difference? I would suggest that he can, if he's the right man, and I believe my selection is. His sales numbers, which are phenomenal—though he has been hampered by his past employer—speak for themselves, and we are going to give him the opportunity to use his full skill set to help grow our business. He won't accomplish this growth single handedly. It will take all of us working together to realize our true potential as a major player in the markets we serve."

"Come on, Jonathan," Charles interjected, "you're holding us all in suspense. Who is this guy?" Jonathan smiled.

Meanwhile, the Landover parking lot was heating up. After a long pause, Jack managed to speak, as he once again raised his hands in a gesture of innocence. "Daniel, please. Let's go somewhere and discuss this rationally. Surely, we can—"

"Rational?" Daniel interrupted, leaning forward on his toes. "You want to be rational? You sure you mean rational, Jack, and not contractual? I know," Daniel offered, "what if we just make ourselves an agreement right here in the parking lot, an agreement like you made with my father. And, hey, what if you give me a nice gift, too, so I'll accept your lame silence as a sign of true concern for my needs, with no questions asked? You know, like the gift you gave my father. In fact, what if I was to offer you that gift right now and give you what you truly deserve?"

Just as Jack noticed Daniel's right hand being raised from his overcoat, he squeezed his eyes closed, gritted his teeth, and tightened every muscle in his body, knowing what was coming next.

Don't let it hurt, don't let it hurt! Jack said to himself.

Cheryl moved her hand over her phone, anticipating needing to call the police. Bill and Jerry both leaned forward on the balls of their feet, assuming Jack and Daniel were about to start fighting.

Daniel moved his hand to the side of his face and scratched his jaw, amused at Jack's cowardice.

Everyone at Cheryl's desk sighed in relief, as Bill and Jerry leaned back flat on their feet.

Daniel leaned his head over to position his lips as close as he could to Jack's left ear without touching him.

"Is he, I mean, it looks like …I think he's going to kiss him," Jerry said.

"Ooh, no way," Cheryl said.

Just as Daniel had maneuvered his mouth in position, he yelled, "BOOM!" As soon as Jack heard the noise, he just knew he had been shot in the head. His legs immediately went numb as his body crumpled to the pavement, striking his head, and knocking him out, and he lay there motionless.

Cheryl stood to her feet and all three took a couple of steps closer to the window.

"What did he do," Cheryl asked.

"I don't know," Bill replied. "I didn't see anyone throw a punch."

"Maybe he tripped again," Jerry offered. Bill and Cheryl looked at Jerry, as if he had been watching a different confrontation.

"I'd better go see what's going on," Bill said, as he made his way out the door and into the parking lot.

"Aren't you going with him, Jerry?" Cheryl asked.

"Oh, sure," Jerry responded, as though caught off guard by the question. He set his coffee mug down, repositioned his safety goggles and walked out behind Bill to the parking lot.

"Don't ever come back to our place again," Daniel yelled at Jack, then noticed he wasn't moving. Daniel was stunned. He looked around to see if anyone else had seen what happened and noticed Bill and Jerry approaching him. "What did I do?" he asked, with his elbows at his side and palms turned up, looking to them for absolution.

When Bill got close, he saw a small amount of blood, which suggested Jack may have had a head injury. He looked back at

Jerry and cried, "Call 9-1-1, and hurry!" Jerry ran back into the building to get Cheryl to call.

Daniel backed up to give Bill room, who rushed to Jack's side and knelt beside him to administer first aid. He was able to detect a pulse, and that Jack was breathing on his own but was afraid to move him until medical help arrived. After confirming Cheryl had made the 9-1-1 call, Jerry returned to the group. Realizing there was little else he could do, Bill looked up to Daniel and asked, "Who are you, and what happened?"

"Daniel!" a voice bellowed from across the parking lot. It was Albert, who just arrived and came running to him. Bill heard the voice and watched the vaguely familiar man approach.

Tom had just pulled into the parking lot and noticed the small group gathered around the man on the ground. He ran over to offer his assistance. "Is there anything I can—" Tom stopped in mid-sentence, as he looked around at the familiar faces on the scene. "Albert?"

"Tom," Albert replied.

"Daniel?"

"Hey, Tom," Daniel responded.

"Tom?" Bill asked. "Who are you?"

"I'm Tom Brandent, the new Landover salesman."

"You work for Landover now?" Daniel asked.

"Yes! Today's my first day. I'm sorry I couldn't say anything before."

"I'm Bill Redding," Bill interjected, "President of Landover."

"Sorry I'm late," Tom said. "Is there anything I can do? I'm trained in first aid."

"I think he struck his head on the pavement when he fell and knocked himself out. From what I can tell, he appears to just be unconscious, but I'm afraid to move him because of his apparent head injury. We have emergency personnel on their way. In the meantime," Bill continued, as he stood to his feet, being sure to offer Jack's face as much shade as he could, and looking at Daniel, "I'd like to know what's going on."

"Daniel, did you do this?" Albert asked.

"I didn't touch him, Dad, I promise," Daniel protested, holding both hands in front of him.

"Where's the gun?" Albert demanded.

When Bill, Tom and Jerry heard the word, gun, they each took a step back.

"What gun? I don't have a gun."

"The gun you took from my desk," Albert barked. "Where is it?"

"I took that gun and put it in my desk to keep it from you."

"Then, what did you do to Jack?"

"Jack?" Tom asked. "Who's Jack?"

"Jack Fisher, the guy on the ground," Albert explained.

"That's Jack Fisher?" Tom asked.

"Yeah, that's Jack Fisher," Daniel replied. "The little coward!"

"Daniel!" Albert called out, becoming more frustrated. "What did you do to Jack?"

"I didn't do anything to him. He thought I had a gun and that I was going to shoot him."

"Did you tell him you had a gun?" Bill asked.

"I didn't tell him any such thing. He just assumed I did."

"Then how did he end up on the ground?" Bill responded.

Daniel rolled his eyes back as he began his explanation to Bill. "Jack and I were arguing about the deal he had scammed my father into agreeing to."

"Watch your mouth, Son," Albert countered.

Daniel looked at Albert and said, "I'm sorry, Dad, but you know it's true." Albert gave a short stare at Daniel then hung his head. Daniel continued his explanation to Bill. "I called Jack a lying snake and only made a reference to the gift he had given my father, which was a nine-millimeter pistol. He thought I had it with me and that I was going to shoot him. He closed his eyes and prepared for the worst. I thought it was funny, and wanted to see how he would respond if I just—"

"Just what, Daniel?" Albert inquired.

"I yelled, Boom, in his ear," Daniel replied.

"That's a relief. I thought you kissed him," Jerry commented.

Daniel gave him a stern stare. Jerry checked his safety goggles to be sure they were properly positioned and took a step back.

"Just, Boom?" Bill asked.

"Well," Daniel admitted, "I yelled really loud."

They all stared at Daniel, in the simplicity of what he described, just as the ambulance and police car arrived.

In the Gantly boardroom, Jonathan's moment of triumph had finally arrived. "I know everyone is anxious for me to introduce my new talent, and he should be arriving any moment." Jonathan glanced at his watch and noticed it was 9:00am. "Oh, I think it's that time. Pardon me, everyone, while I check on our new team member." Jonathan stepped out of the boardroom into the first empty office and picked up the phone and called Claire.

"Operator," she answered.

"Claire, please send Mr. Fisher in".

"I'm sorry, Mr. Edwards, Mr. Fisher is not here yet".

"Are you sure, Claire?"

"Yes, Mr. Edwards, I'm sure."

"Please bring him into the boardroom the moment he arrives."

"Yes, sir," she responded.

"Late on your first day, Jack," Jonathan said. "Not a good start." Jonathan made his way back to the boardroom, where everyone waited to see who was coming in with him. They were surprised when Jonathan entered alone and closed the door behind him. "It appears our new addition is running a little behind. I'm sure he's on his way. If you will please bear with me for just a few moments longer."

The medical technicians gathered their gear and rushed to Jack's side. Everyone else stood back to give the technicians as much room as they needed to do their job. As the group watched with concern, the police officers joined them to perform their scene investigation.

"Okay," the first officer said, "who can tell me what happened here?"

Bill was the first to speak up. "Officer, my name is Bill Redding, President of Landover."

"Let's step over here, sir," the policeman requested, desiring to split the group up for questioning. The second officer took Daniel and Albert off the other direction. Jerry wondered off to the ambulance while Tom stood alone, out of everyone's way.

Once they had taken a few steps, Bill continued his description as the officer opened his pad and started taking notes. "The man on the ground is, or was, one of our salesmen, Jack Fisher."

"What do you mean, he was your salesman? Is he dead?" Before Bill could answer, the officer looked over at the medical technician and called, "Hey Phillip! Is that guy dead?"

"Oh, no, Jay," Phillip replied. "He may have a minor head contusion and possible concussion, but I think he'll be okay. Though he appears to be unconscious, he has tried to move his limbs."

"So, if he's not dead," the officer continued with Bill, "then why do you say he was your salesman?"

"I just fired him last week, so he doesn't work for me anymore."

"Got it. Now, who all was involved in the altercation?"

"There were only two people out here: Jack Fisher, and that gentleman over there with the other officer."

"Do you know his name?"

"From here it looks like his badge reads, Officer Millwood?"

"Not the officer's name, sir, the name of the other participant in the altercation."

"Oh, I'm sorry. I believe his name is Daniel."

"And you said you saw what happened?"

"Yes. We witnessed what happened from the lobby window. We were standing—"

"We?" the officer interrupted. "So, there were other witnesses, too?"

"Yes. Myself, Jerry Simpson, our safety director, and Cheryl Jameson, our receptionist."

"Are these other people out here?"

"Cheryl is still inside, answering the phones, and Jerry is standing over there next to the ambulance, admiring all the gadgetry."

The officer looked over at Jerry and then asked Bill, "Did this incident compromise your chemical lab?

"Chemical lab?" Bill responded.

"Do you have a chemical lab here?"

"No," Bill replied. "Why do you ask?"

"Never mind," he said. "It must be something about safety guys and goggles. Go ahead and tell me what you saw." Jerry left the ambulance and walked up to Bill just as he started his description of the incident.

"We were all standing in the lobby looking out the window and watching all this unfold. Jack was carrying a box of his belongings to his car and apparently tripped and dropped his box. While he was gathering his things, Daniel approached him. We couldn't hear what was being said, but it was obvious from the body language they were having a heated argument."

"He looked aggressive," Jerry interjected. The officer glanced over at Jerry, and then turned back to Bill.

"Jack stood up," Bill continued, "and Daniel was really getting in his face when all of a sudden it appeared Daniel positioned his mouth very close to Jack's ear."

"Yeah, I thought he was going to kiss him," Jerry once again interjected. The officer gave Jerry a quick bewildered look.

"Again," Bill went on, "we couldn't tell what Daniel did, because all we could see was the back of his head. Daniel claims he just yelled, Boom, in Jack's ear and he crumpled to the ground."

"Boom?" the officer asked.

"Yes, just, Boom".

"Were there any punches thrown, or did Daniel touch Jack in any way?"

"Not that we could see."

"Okay. I think I've got what I need. Do you know any next-of-kin that should be notified of Mr. Fisher's condition?"

"Yes. I'll call his wife and let her know."

"Thank you for your help, Mr. Redding." The officer walked over to his partner to help finish up the preliminary investigation.

In the meantime, the medical technicians had assessed Jack's condition, bandaged his head, and laid him on a gurney. Jack drifted in and out of consciousness before they loaded him in the ambulance. Before the ambulance left, Bill asked one of the technicians, "Is he going to be okay?"

"His heart and respiratory rates show normal, given the circumstances, and he has tried to move around a little, but he's semi-conscious, or at least very groggy. He's lost a little blood, but not a whole lot. It looks like he struck his head on something on the pavement when he got knocked out. Hopefully, it's just a concussion."

"Do you know what he struck?" Bill inquired.

"We found an object directly under his head, which is probably what cut his scalp. We'll be taking it to the hospital with us just in case there is a need for further investigation. We'll get him to the emergency room, and you'll be able to get more information there."

"Where are you taking him," Bill asked.

"We'll take him to Glenden Heights Hospital over on Miner Boulevard."

"Thanks," Bill replied, as the technicians entered the ambulance and sped away.

The second officer had just finished his questioning of Daniel. "Mr. Torres, I'm going to ask that you stay in town, close to home, until this matter is resolved. Mr. Fisher may want to file some charges against you. Do you understand?"

"Yes, sir," Daniel answered. "I'm not going anywhere, so don't worry."

The two officers returned to their squad car and left the facility. "I'm sorry for all the commotion, Bill," Albert offered.

"I appreciate that, Albert. Let's just hope and pray Jack will be okay."

"I'll say. Daniel and I are going to get back to work. Please let us know if there's anything we can do to help."

As Daniel and Albert drove away, Tom, Jerry and Bill were left alone in the parking lot. Several other Landover employees were either watching from inside the lobby or standing at the front entryway. Bill walked over to Tom and offered his hand to properly introduce himself. "Tom, I'm Bill Redding, President of Landover." He pointed back to the accident scene. "This isn't the norm around here, but what a way to start your first day."

"It has certainly been exciting so far," Tom said.

With Jerry close by, Bill introduced him to Tom. "This is Jerry Simpson, our Safety Director."

"Jerry, it's my pleasure to meet you."

"It's good to meet you, too, Tom."

"It looks like this thing caught you in the middle of a training class," Tom suggested.

"Oh no, I was just drinking a cup of coffee in the lobby."

"That coffee must be some stout stuff if you have to wear safety goggles to drink it."

"Oh, these things?" Jerry asked, reaching for his goggles, and removing them. "I just keep forgetting I have them on."

"Come on in," Bill offered. "I need to call Jack's wife, Paula, and let her know what has happened and, then I'll find Paul

Grissom for you. He can show you around the facility."

"I'll get Jack's things and bring them inside," Jerry offered.

"Thanks, Jerry," Bill replied. As they made their way to the building, Bill looked up toward the front entrance and saw a few employees still standing there. "Alright, everybody, let's get back to work. The show's over." He and Tom walked into the lobby and approached the receptionist's desk. "Cheryl," Bill called, as they reached her desk.

"How's Jack? Is he going to be okay?"

"They think he may have a concussion, but it looks like he'll be okay. We'll learn more later."

"That sounds encouraging."

"I'd like you to meet Tom …I'm sorry," he said as he turned to Tom, "what did you say your last name was?"

"Brandent, Tom Brandent," Tom replied.

"I'd like you to meet Tom Brandent," Bill repeated to Cheryl. Then turning to Tom, "Tom, this is Cheryl, our receptionist." The two exchanged pleasantries. "Tom is our new equipment salesman."

"Boy," she said, "that was quick," referring to Jack's apparent successor.

Bill snickered while Tom looked perplexed. He escorted Tom to his office and invited him in. "Just have a seat, Tom, and I'll be with you right after I call Paula." He took his place behind his desk and scrolled through his phone numbers until he found Jack's home number. He dialed the number, hoping she would be home. "Hello, Paula Fisher? Mrs. Fisher, this is Bill Redding with Landover. I wanted to call and inform you of a situation involving your husband, Jack." Tom sat there, feeling a little uncomfortable listening to the conversation, thankful he couldn't hear her responses. "There's been an accident here in our parking lot. Jack had an altercation with another man and has fallen and knocked himself out. I really don't know any more than that, except the ambulance has taken him to Glenden Heights Hospital, over on Miner Boulevard. He did appear to be okay, at least as far as the medical technicians could determine, but he appeared to be unconscious, or at least very groggy." Bill listened to Paula's comments, and then added, "Your welcome. Please call if there is anything we can do to help." Bill hung up the phone.

"Man," Bill said, sounding exhausted, "this has already started out as a busy week. You're probably wondering what you've gotten yourself into, aren't you?" Bill asked.

"It has been a little different, that's for sure. So that was Jack Fisher?" Tom asked.

"Yes, it was. Do you know him?"

"Only by reputation. I was an equipment salesman at Gantly for six years and, as you would probably guess, he and I have gone head-to-head for about the last two years competing for much of the same business. I was anxious to meet him this morning, and I look forward to working with him."

"I'm afraid that's not going to happen," Bill said, a little disappointed.

"You're telling me. It'll probably be a few days before he's back to work. I guess I'll have to wait to meet him."

"I'm sorry, Tom," Bill said, a little embarrassed. "I should have told you earlier. I fired Jack last week. He came in this morning just to pick up the last of his personal belongings, so he won't be coming back." Tom raised his eyebrows, shocked at the news.

"That's very surprising, Mr. Redding. From all that I had seen from the outside, Jack was doing a great job."

"He was. Jack's a great salesman, and I'm sure he'll do a great job for his next employer. I know you probably have a thousand questions, and rightfully so, especially after a morning like this, but I don't have time to discuss any details regarding his dismissal. I can tell you we pride ourselves on running a business above reproach, and it cost something when we violate the underlying moral and ethical principles that comprise our foundation. I know that's a mouthful, Tom, and I hope I'm not scaring you off."

"Oh no, Mr. Redding, I understand your position. I wish every company had such a business philosophy." *Every company*, he thought.

"Great! If you'll wait right here, I'll go get Paul for you. They have a sales meeting every Monday morning, and they're usually out by now." Bill glanced at his watch. "It's 9:10. I wonder what's taking them." Bill rose from his chair. "I'll be right back," he said, as he headed off to the boardroom.

Bill knocked on the boardroom door and stuck his head in just as the meeting was breaking up. "Hey, Paul. Tom's here."

"Man, that was fast. I didn't expect him to get here until lunch." Paul looked at Ben and Tony. "Just hang around here guys for a few more minutes. There's someone I'd like for you to meet. I'll be right back."

Paul followed Bill to his office. When Paul walked in, Tom's face lit up, as he recognized his new friend and stood to greet him. "Good morning, Mr. Grissom, it's good to see you again."

"Please, Tom, call me Paul. It's great to have you on board! I must say, I didn't expect to see you show up so soon this morning, but it's good that you did. I see you have already met Bill, our President."

"Yes, he and I met in the parking lot after Jack Fisher fell."

"Jack fell in the parking lot?" Paul asked, looking at Bill.

"I don't think it's anything serious," Bill responded. "He had a confrontation in the parking lot with Daniel, Albert Torres's son, and he fell and knocked himself out for a little while. We called 9-1-1 and the ambulance came and took him to Glenden Heights Hospital. I'll fill you in about it later."

"Maybe we'll go by the hospital later and see how he's doing." Then turning to Tom, "Are you ready to start your career at Landover?" he asked smiling.

"Yes, sir," Tom answered with excitement.

"Then let's head back to the boardroom and I'll introduce you to the rest of the sales team. We'll get your application paperwork taken care of later."

In the Gantly boardroom, the snacks were all gone, and everyone had run out of patience and broken up into small groups engaged in idle chit-chat. Jonathan rehearsed his sales exploits of days-gone-by to Ray and Cliff, who listened only out of courtesy, while Charles kept Lisa, Jeffery and Lou intrigued with his family's travel experiences. Darrell just sat there listening to it all, wondering if this meeting was going to break up anytime soon, so he could go back to work. The room grew silent when Claire paged Jonathan to the phone the second time. "Here you go Jonathan," Charles said. "This is it."

Jonathan smiled as he once again exited the boardroom and picked up the phone in a nearby empty office. "Sales, this is Jonathan," he answered.

"Mr. Edwards, this is Paula Fisher, Jack's wife."

"Oh, yes, Mrs. Fisher. Is there something wrong?"

"Mr. Edwards, Jack was involved in some kind of situation at Landover before he left there this morning and fell and hit his head."

"Is he alright?"

"They've brought him here to Glenden Heights Hospital over on Miner Boulevard. The doctor said he'll be okay, but he's still very groggy from the fall. They've given him some medication and requested that he stay overnight for observation. I know he was supposed to start his new job today, and he'll feel terrible having let you down."

"Quite the contrary, Mrs. Fisher," Jonathan assured her. "Jack's health is what's important. Just tell him to take care of himself and join us when he's ready. We're all excited to have him on our team and look forward to working with him."

"Thank you, Mr. Edwards. I'll call you if anything changes."

Jonathan hung up the phone, pleased that Jack was okay. "Well, my boy, it's good to know you're still on board." He released a deep sigh of relief. "This is going to take the thunder out of my morning presentation." He picked up the phone and called Claire.

"Operator."

"Claire, the young man I asked you to look out for this morning, Jack Fisher, has been involved in an accident and is currently at the Glenden Heights Hospital over on Miner Boulevard. Please send him some flowers with a get-well card."

"Yes, sir, Mr. Edwards. By the way, Mr. Edwards, I tried calling Tom Brandent on his cell phone and got a very strange recording. It's Tom's voice but he is directing all callers to our main number."

"What do you mean, all callers?" Jonathan asked.

"His message greeting says something about how his cell phone messages are not monitored, and anyone wishing to get in touch with him should call our main number."

"I'll be right there. I'd like to hear it myself." Jonathan hung up the phone and walked to Claire's desk. Once he arrived, she handed him one of her headsets so he could listen in on the call, as she dialed Tom's cell phone. When the phone rang, Jonathan could faintly hear what he thought sounded like the distinct ringtone of Tom's phone coming from one of the offices close by. In the middle of the second ring, Jonathan laid the headset down on the desk and followed the sound of the faint ring. It directed him to Tom's office, where he arrived at the beginning of the fourth ring. Jonathan looked in and discovered Tom's phone, credit card and ID badge laying on his desk, which had also been cleared of all personal items. He rushed back to Claire's desk, where she was listening to the voice message and holding the second handset up for Jonathan.

"If you hurry you can catch the last of the message," she informed him.

"Never mind, Claire. May I see the letter Tom left behind, please?"

"It's almost over," she said, urging him to listen.

"Claire, the letter, please." Claire hung up the phone, took the letter from Jonathan's mail slot and handed it to him. "Thank you." He opened the letter while walking back toward the boardroom. About halfway down the hall, Jonathan stopped to finish reading the letter. "The little worm!" he muttered. "This is how he repays me? He has no idea what he has given up! And to think I was going to make him my number two salesman."

"Jonathan," Charles called, standing outside the boardroom. Jonathan snapped his head at the sound of Charles's voice. "Let's get this thing wrapped up so everyone can get back to work."

"Be right there, Charles," Jonathan responded.

Chapter 18

At Landover, the details of Jack's accident had spread throughout the company, and many were concerned. Bill had been sure to stay in touch with Paula, so when he came back from lunch, he had the latest update. When he walked through the front door, he saw Carl at the receptionist's desk. "Hey, Carl. What are you up to?"

"I'm just up here fiddlin' around, about to get off my lunch break."

"Cheryl, I've got some more news about Jack. He's still unconscious but all the tests have come back negative, so they expect him to be just fine once he wakes up and has a few days of rest. They're going to keep him in the hospital overnight as a precaution."

"That's great! I'll be sure to pass the word along to anyone that calls me."

"Thanks, Cheryl. I'll see you later, Carl," Bill said, as he walked back to his office.

"That's a relief," Cheryl declared.

"Yep, Jack is one lucky man," Carl responded. "It could've been much worse. It's a good thing he's got a wife to be with him."

"Speaking of wives, or women in general, how did your and Jerry's weekend go?" Cheryl asked.

"Weekend? We spent one afternoon together, not the whole weekend. And how did that tie into women?"

"Wasn't that the reason for you two to meet? So how did it go?"

"It was just fine. We watched a little television, ate, and talked for a while. Jerry's a lot different man when he's away from work. I don't think he wore those goggles once all the time I was there."

"That's encouraging," Cheryl said. "What did ya'll talk about?"

"I didn't say too much, except I told him I wasn't in the market for another woman at the moment, since I already had my eye on one." Carl laughed as Cheryl shook her head. "But Jerry went on and on about some girl he knows or wants to know. He had something to say about almost every feature she had." Carl began to scan Cheryl's face. "From her golden-brown hair to her deep, baby-blue eyes, to her rosy, red lips. You know, I would almost bet he was referring to—"

"Hey, Carl," Jerry called out, as he approached the receptionist's desk. "Hi, Cheryl," he said with a smile. "Thanks for coming over, Saturday, Carl. It was a lot of fun."

"You did fix a mighty good meal. Those steaks were great, and I hated to leave that last bit of homemade coconut pie." He gave Cheryl a nod of approval.

"Cheryl," Jerry started timidly, "I was wondering if you would like to—"

"Wow, Jerry, you bake?" Cheryl asked, as though she didn't hear him.

"Not as good as my mother," he responded, "but I know my way around an oven. Every bachelor should know how to take care of himself, including knowing how to cook. So, Cheryl—"

"You would think so," Cheryl said, staring at Carl.

"I can cook anything on the grill," Carl responded. "I just

don't do any baking. Now, my momma is a baker."

"She sure is," Cheryl agreed.

Jerry looked at Cheryl. "You know Carl's mother?"

"Just like my mother," she added, again, not addressing Jerry's question.

"Yep," Carl replied. Surprised, Jerry stood speechless. "The stories of them two trying to out cook one another when they were younger are legendary."

"So, your mom and Cheryl's mom—"

"The two best cooks in Denton County. I guess I better be gettin' on back to work. My break's about over." Carl started to leave and then caught himself. "Did you need me for somethin', Jerry?"

"Oh no. I was looking for Cheryl, to ask her something," he answered. "But I don't want to hold you up, Carl, if you need to get back to work."

"I still got a few minutes yet." Carl glanced at his watch and stood still.

After a short pause, and sensing Carl wasn't going anywhere, Jerry continued. "I think the answer just came to me."

"What was the question, Jerry?" Cheryl asked.

"It's not that important, now. I was just wondering if you would …like to …maybe, if you had time …" he glanced over at Carl, who was grinning ear to ear, "if you liked the spreadsheet I sent you earlier this morning."

"Sure, Jerry. It worked fine."

"Okay. That's great. I guess I better get back to work." Jerry turned and walked away, as Cheryl and Carl looked at each other and shrugged their shoulders.

Several hours later, Jack was still unconscious but resting. Paula sat alone by his bed watching the television, waiting for him to wake up.

At about 3:00pm Jack's breathing changed as he began to move his body a little, indicating he was becoming conscious. Paula was immediately at his side. "Jack? Jack, honey, are you awake?"

"Huh," he said, trying to open his eyes, still groggy from the fall and the medication.

"Jack, it's me, Paula. You're okay, honey."

"Am I in heaven?" Jack asked in a weak voice with his eyes still closed.

"No, honey," she giggled.

"Oh no! I'm in—"

"You're in the hospital," she said.

Jack began rolling his head around and trying to hold his eyes open. "Am I going to die?" he asked.

"Are you going to what?" Paula responded with a curious look.

"Die," he tried to say louder, but his diminished strength wouldn't allow him. "Am I going to die?" Jack said, finally able to hold his eyes open, though squinting. "You know: buy the farm, kick the bucket, crossover to the other side."

"Who told you that?"

"Most people that get shot in the head die from their wounds, don't they?"

"You didn't get shot in the head, silly."

"Then why does it hurt so badly?" he asked with a little more strength.

"You fell in the parking lot and hit your head. You have a mild concussion" Jack's face expressed a bewildered look.

"I did what?"

"You fell in the parking lot and hit your head," she repeated.

"No," Jack argued. "That's not what happened." He closed his eyes, trying to relive the incident. "The last thing I remember, he reached for his gun and pointed it—"

"There was no gun," Paula interrupted.

Jack turned to Paula with child-like innocence, "Sure there

211

was. He pointed it at my head and then pulled—"

"Jack," she said, "there was no gun."

Jack lay still for a moment. "Are you saying I didn't get shot?"

"Yes, you didn't get shot. You just fell."

"Then, what was the loud noise I heard?"

"It was some awful guy named Daniel. The police officer said he told them you had your eyes closed because you thought he was going to shoot you, and that's when he yelled in your ear just to scare you. I guess it stunned you and caused you to fall and hit your head." Jack lay there puzzled with this new information, not sure what to believe.

"But his hand," he started, still grasping for words, "his hand looked like he had something in it. When I looked down at his hand in his pocket, I was sure I saw …his hand!" He closed his eyes, a little embarrassed. "What an idiot I am!"

"You're not an idiot. Most people would have reacted the same way."

"You mean most people without a backbone," he said, turning his head away from Paula.

"Don't beat yourself up. At least you're still alive," she said, trying to encourage him.

"Yeah, but for how long?" he asked, as he looked up to the ceiling.

"Oh, get a grip, Jack," Paula said, a little annoyed. "So, you can't handle the thought of death. Neither can I."

"You can't?" Jack asked, surprised, knowing she was the emotionally strong one.

"In fact, I think most people feel uncomfortable to imagine what may await them on the other side. It may be best for us to not think about it and just be thankful we can live another day. You're no more afraid than anyone else is."

"Thanks, Paula." Paula leaned over the bed and kissed Jack on the forehead. "Ouch, that hurt," he grimaced.

"Oh, you big baby." Jack smiled.

"By the way, what did I hit my head on?"

"The doctor said it was this blunt object he gave me," Paula answered, as she walked over to her purse. "By the way, Paul came by around lunch time."

"That sounds like Paul. He's a good man. Was anyone with him?"

"He was with Bill and some new guy I've never seen before," she replied, still searching her purse. "He introduced him as their new salesman, Tom Brandent."

New salesman, huh. Boy, that didn't take long. They must've had this planned before they even fired me!

"I guess they hired him to take your place after you quit."

"Yeah," he responded. "They probably did." *I wonder how long this has been in the works.*

"Here it is." Paula brought the object over to Jack and handed it to him. "I cleaned it up a little. It had blood all over it." He took hold of it and knew right away what it was.

"My SOTY!" Despite the methods he employed to achieve it, the accolade was still special to him. "How ironic," he said, as he rotated the piece with his hands, examining every facet. "My last sale to Torres Construction made this possible."

"Can you see it okay, hon?"

"Oh yes," he said, his eyes still fastened on his trophy. "I'm beginning to see everything clear …crystal clear."

"Do you need anything? Are you hungry?"

"Not right now," Jack answered. "I'm still a little tired."

"Now that I know you're okay, do you mind if I step out for a little bit and come back later this evening?"

"Oh no. I know you've been up here all day, and I'm sure you've got some things you need to do. I'll be okay."

"I'll bring you back something to eat."

"That will be great," he smiled. Paula gave Jack a kiss and gathered her purse.

"Did you want me to put that thing back in my purse?"

"I'll hold on to it for now," Jack answered.

When he heard the door close, Jack clinched his award,

closed his eyes, and turned toward the wall. He sensed moisture gathering in the corner of his eye and felt it run across the bridge of his nose and drip on his pillow. "This is not how change is supposed to work," he said. "This is my life! I decide!"

ABOUT THE AUTHOR

RK Brumbalow has spent over four decades involved with the off-road, industrial equipment business and interacted with the people that build, service, and sell industrial equipment. He uses his experience to capture some of the human side of the business and the often-eccentric idiosyncrasies of us all.